LEBANON, LEBANON

LEBANON, LEBANON

Edited by
Anna Wilson

SAQI
London   San Francisco

The proceeds from the book will go
to children's charities in Lebanon.

ISBN (10): 0-86356-641-3
ISBN (13): 978-0-86356-641-7

Published in 2006 by Saqi Books

Manufactured in the United Kingdom by CPI

C P I
United Kingdom

SAQI

26 Westbourne Grove, London W2 5RH
825 Page Street, Suite 203, Berkeley, California 94710
www.saqibooks.com

This book is dedicated
to the memory of
our dear friend and colleague
Ali Barq
1966–2006

Acknowledgements

Our thanks to the contributors, who each offered their work free of charge and who all responded at lightening speed to our request.

Thanks also to all those who provided translations for no fee: Issa J. Boullata, Catherine Cobham, Yasmine Gaspard, Amal Ghandour, Cullen Goldblatt and Hassan Ramadan.

Special thanks to Mitch Albert, Maureen Ali, Anthony Barnett, Julia Bird, Lynn Gaspard, Maggie Gee, Jana Gough, Andy Hull, Alberto Manguel, Jan Michael, Els van der Plas, Lucy Popescu, Nick Smith, Richard Stanton and Judith Vidal-Hall.

Thanks to all the publishers and agents who helped in so many ways to get this project off the ground.

Thanks to the CPI Group for contributing the 8-page colour section, free of charge.

Thanks to the anonymous donor who paid for the printing costs.

Thanks to Al Jana and all the volunteers and children involved in the Masrah al-Madina project.

And finally, we salute Dina Dally and everyone at Dar al Saqi in Beirut for all their dedication and courage, and for getting books out of Lebanon against all the odds.

Texts

Illustrations

Colour illustrations *(between pages 128–129)*

Harold Pinter

American Football

Hallelullah!
It works.
We blew the shit out of them.

We blew the shit right back up their own ass
And out their fucking ears.

It works.
We blew the shit out of them.
They suffocated in their own shit!

Hallelullah.
Praise the Lord for all good things.

We blew them into fucking shit.
They are eating it.

Praise the Lord for all good things.

We blew their balls into shards of dust,
Into shards of fucking dust.

We did it.

Now I want you to come over here and kiss
    me on the mouth.

Abbas Beydoun

A Possible Poem on Dahiya

I don't know any poet who has written a poem on Dahiya, and I don't think that a poem singing about its destruction is ever possible. We will surely read rhymes and metres, but who will give them any attention? The eyes that the rockets have opened in Dahiya's buildings will, for a long time, remain eyes with a dreadful look, which poets will never dare to encounter. They will never know what to do with a broken rib of concrete, how to see a fallen wing of hard cement, how to contemplate those volumes of stone stacked over one another. Worse still, they will be afraid of those architectural dinosaurs that disappeared without a scream. And, of course, they will be unable to find a rhyme for the endless odyssey of rubble; for the tsunami of debris and its waves tumbling over one another; for the quivering sails on the tops of buildings; for the stone tatters caught in the throes of death on the roofs; and for the vast wasteland that appeared all of a sudden … 'Where can we find a rhyme of this magnitude,' asks a poet accustomed to garden roses. 'Where can we find the metre for this earthquake?' The poet will understandably look for a blade of grass in the cracks, for a handkerchief, a tasselled carpet, a rosary, a broken walking stick; but there are no suitable words to calculate the immensity of earthquakes, planetary explosions, and outbursts of nature.

Poets and those who are not poets can note that this unnamed city,[1] which mostly spoke in the language of huge measurements and large sizes, was not heard by anyone. We don't know whether it spoke to poets or thought of them. This unnamed city did not ask poets for a single word; and when it had to choose one, it found for itself the word that had been lost from their dictionary. It was not a question of words. The hatred of the first mother and of the second mother, and the broken spirit of the father, were a conjuncture of suffering treated secretly and away from everyone's eyes. Through the act of forgetting came the great unconsciousness, and in this unconsciousness – perhaps from it – were born the mountains of stone and cement; giants of heavy rubble came into being. Cities rose from the needs of other cities, from the lies of other cities, and from the deceit of other cities. In this unconsciousness, a reality light years from its own selfhood came into being. Places born of separations which can only bear their pains by more separations, and places born of a trauma which can only be treated by a measure of invisibility – such places have no language, of course.

Unnamed, we lived – on an unnamed land in an unnamed existence – to hate other cities, to worship other cities. We had no power and were at a loss regarding a dead mother, a paradise that started like a mother, a father whose headdress and moustache had collapsed before becoming a father himself.

---

1.   *Dahiya* in Arabic means suburb. This suburb of Beirut remained unnamed, and its proper name came to be Dahiya (*Translator*).

We were suddenly fathers ourselves; we were men ourselves, hating an impotent tenderness and the suffering of a scorned manhood. The lost name became unnamed, and the hated world became vacant. We were the surplus of cities, the surplus of life, the surplus of human beings, the surplus of overcrowding. And here, where no one had specific features, we had to move without faces in an undetermined and an unlimited nebulous existence. Here, there was nothing but a place among places. Around us there arose markets of necessity, schools of necessity, minarets of necessity – and we did not notice. Not a single thing existed so that we might perceive it, not a single thing spoke to us – except a plant in our heads, a strange salamander that ascribed itself to us from the extremity of the world.

No poet has written on Dahiya. Can a poet say anything about ruined spaces that need topographers, astronomers, city-planners, cineastes, computers more than they need poets? The place consists of heaps upon heaps; of plains of ruined heaps. Can we be deviant and speak about beauty here? Or is the real ruin on our tongues? For in this stretched-out unconsciousness, there is no word for what has now been transformed into a featureless, shapeless heap. Can we speak of a lost history, when we have not been aware of history until now, when we see it collapsed? Can we now remember what has occurred, as an insignificant repetition? Can we now think in language's terms about something we had given neither a name nor qualities? Let us at least see …

We are surprised both when we see this heaped rubble, and when we don't see it again. We are surprised at the immense horror but we don't weep. The tear of remorse, if it exists, is bigger than a rock and it will crush us. Perhaps in the next millennium, we will learn how to be normal, how to love our mothers whether they are beautiful or not, how to love ourselves and not fall into the narcissism of our scorned manhood, how to have a home, a homeland, a life of our own.

Like all the people who lived in Dahiya or did not, I left something in it, a root worth neither a mention nor an appearance, a root that is not counted among roots. Here, there was princely talk, a dining table, drinking with friends, the leftist adventure; here, there were scores of men and their fragrant tobacco smoke, and the unnamed freedoms; here, there was the love of overcrowding, of being lost, of wandering about in the streets and neighbourhoods; and here, there were people, there was hospitality. There was something for me in that place: a shirt here, a piece of leather there. It was predestined for us to forget Dahiya in order to become men. It was predestined for us to hate it instead of ourselves. We did not return often to Dahiya. Some of us began to talk about the crowding, the potholes, and other things. We entered the realm of reciprocal forgetfulness and mutual isolation. Nihilistic things were being born from other nihilistic things, and there was no need for remorse.

The heaps and the rubble fall in our memories too and in our inner selves. We say: let us only continue the wound of our life, the disease of reality here, where it is possible for misery to become a style, where we have learned how to be healed. No one is now asking for atonement, because the doors here don't shut out anybody, because we always have a first priority, not only when we die, not only when our friends die. We have here our letters of mud and our aesthetics of crowding. We have names on the stones, and we have stones that have fallen as names. We have here a surplus of life, a surplus of concrete, where walls have no mothers, and where walls are not a family. We have here homes that are never too cramped, we have doors that shut out nobody. We have something we left in the middle of the newspaper, in the middle of the room, in the opening of the bottle. We have homes made of a chair and a dining table with one dish. No one is asking for atonement in this place, which is our life – and the doors don't shut out anybody.

Translated by Issa J. Boullata

Hassan Daoud

They Destroy and We Build

The switch from peace to a state of war is the fastest transition of all. The few minutes leading up to 9.20 am on Tuesday were a world away from the minutes that followed it. There had been no warning … none of the usual signs that war was about to break out. On Tuesday, most Lebanese were contentedly reflecting on the steady rise in the number of tourists flocking to the country. Two days previously, the minister of tourism had announced, 'This year, the figure will reach 1.3 million.' The streets were filled with cars displaying banners bearing the names of all the countries whose inhabitants were coming to Lebanon to spend their holidays. There was no warning. The annual influx of expatriate Lebanese to their homeland for the months of July and August had begun in earnest. Before arriving, many of these homeward-bound expats had asked their relatives and friends to reserve tickets for the Fairuz concerts due to begin on 14 July. Seats had sold out more than a month ago. Now, focusing on the trivial to avoid addressing the more fateful developments unfolding around us, we wonder what all these would-be concert-goers are going to do with their worthless tickets.

Sleeping & Waking-up

In the space of a single day, everything changed. The crowds on Verdun Street have vanished into thin air and the chaotic uproar that emanated from its coffee shops during the World Cup has faded into silence. Indolence and fear are writ clear on the faces of the Amore Cafe's few remaining patrons. The inhabitants of Lebanon's south, who until Tuesday must have thought that the days of artillery bombardment and internal migration were over, have reclaimed their familiar postures on our television screens: trudging along country roads and stumbling across bombed-out bridges with their scant possessions stuffed into small suitcases and nylon holdalls. The most frequently heard remark on Hizbullah's abduction of two Israeli soldiers (the pretext for the bombardment that followed) is 'bad timing'. This diplomatic phrase allows the speaker to avoid an open declaration of disgust at the kidnap operation, in case any Hizbullah supporters happen to be within earshot. Even the politicians and commentators who appear on television make a big point about timing and the need to take an almost limitless number of factors into consideration before acting. To talk about bad timing is to position oneself between those who carried out the operation and the 14 April coalition who issued a statement opposing the abduction because of the destructive retribution it has provoked. In other words, they support the kidnapping but would have preferred it to have been put off to a later date, when the tourists and holiday-makers had gone home.

This call for a 'delay' – although described in a slightly caricatured fashion above – is evidence of Lebanon's implicit acceptance of a seemingly endless vacillation between war and peace. Even worse, it shows that the Lebanese want their peace – when they get it – to be doubly profitable (swelling tourist numbers and frantic rebuilding) while refusing to consign war to the past. Unlike all the other Arab states post-1967, only the Lebanese seem embarrassed to repudiate war.

It is Lebanon's turn to be blessed with peace. The Lebanese talk about 'bad timing' because they are unable to say what they really mean. It's dissimulation and disingenuousness on a mass scale, the only exceptions being those calling openly for war and the gunmen. For many decades now, the latter have called the shots and the results are flattened buildings, gaping holes left by aerial bombardment and footsore refugees fleeing the splintered remnants of their family homes.

This time, the Lebanese are being asked to make the transition from peace to war with a speed even they have never managed before. In a mere twenty-four hours they have been cast back to the hardships of their darkest days. In the blink of an eye the gas stations are crowded with cars, the bakeries are packed with people buying up bread, university examinations are suspended and the front pages carry photographs of a child's body, killed along with the rest of her family during an Israeli bombardment of al-Dweir. The newspapers' coverage of the al-Dweir bombing reminds us of the al-Nabatiyya massacre that took place a few years ago, itself a carbon copy of the al-Mansouri and Qana massacres that so terrified the Lebanese. Such slaughters work in our favour, if only because they bear witness to the barbaric cruelty of the Israelis. This barbarity rears its ugly head time and time again, yet we forget that it causes pain to no one but ourselves. The destruction of our bridges – perhaps all our bridges – in this recent assault could also be seen as in our interests: not only does it provide evidence of Israeli brutality, it also highlights the scandalous lack of response by world leaders.

On Wednesday evening a pro-Hizbullah talking head appeared on TV and stated that everything that the Israelis destroyed could be easily repaired. According to him, houses could be rebuilt and bridges restored by the army engineers. Even as he spoke, Israeli warplanes were loading up to go and destroy more bridges; and the next day and the next, they did exactly that. It was distinctly similar to what one of our top officials said about Israel when he came to office: 'They destroy and we build.' He sounded bizarrely confident – as if the country Israel was destroying and the country we were rebuilding were two different places. Other such examples are plentiful, all showing that the real failure lies not in an inability to express oneself clearly, but in the underlying logic with which years of hardship and horror have made us intimately familiar.

Blake Morrison

Stop

As of today, the peace process will be intensified
through war. These are safe bombs, and any fatalities
will be minors. The targets are strictly military
or civilian. Anomalies may occur, but none
out of the ordinary. This release has been prepared by
official Stop

First reports indicate a major break through
hospital roofs. The bombs were strictly targeted at
random personnel. Any errors are a mere blip
on the radar screen. Until our aim is achieved we will continue
missing. In modern war, mistakes are never made
official Stop

We can confirm that many personnel now enjoy peace,
underground. Several terrorists have been
created overnight. Our smart bombs are subject only to
intelligence errors. Certain one-off tragic events
will regrettably recur. We anticipate a stepping up
of funerals Stop

In another time-zone, the bombs fall unsafely.
There are reports of urgent talk under the rubble.
Numberless children lie accounted for in morgues.
Regrettably, we are unable to offer regrets today.
This poem has been subject to certain restrictions.
Stop.

Rhea

Everything is Connected

Globalization? Mobilization. A world of look-alike puppets. IMF? International Monetary Fund. International Monetary Farce. WTO? World Trade Organization. World Trade? World plunder. Trade what? Humanity for cash? Corporatization? So our lives, wishes, dreams can be owned by the big names. Commercialization ... drops subtle bombs in our minds. Commodification? 'How much air are you intending to breathe today, sir? Right, that will be the usual $20. Next.' Structural adjustments? Few adjustments here, few adjustments there – perfect, all gone, a bulldozer couldn't have done a better job. Global warming? What, you think that might cause a bit of trouble? Nah ... Heatwaves that kill thousands in Europe, floods that kill tens of thousands in India, drought that starves millions in Africa. Tornadoes and hurricanes? They only hit the poor and the black. Oh yeah, and drown cities. Tsunamis? The world is overpopulated anyway; 300,000 less isn't so bad. I don't give a shit. Well ... My TV. My house. My family. My money. My education. My hashish. My cocaine. My computer. My airplane ticket to Sharam El Sheikh. My my. My my. My my.

My my. My my. My my. My my. My my? My life? Is life? Is what? I have, therefore I am? I am. Am what. I am my my, my my, my my, my. Mine. Mine all mine. Me. And you? You? Are who? Are mine. No? You are what I think of you. Mine. All mine. You are what I let you be. Dead. All dead. Buy me. Bargain me. Profit off me. My 'me' is for sale. To whoever can pay the highest price. I am designer. I am designed. By whom? By my blank blank blank products belongings cosmetics cosmopolitan fantasies. Perfection is attainable. I just need one more adjustment. Give it to me.

The origins of 'me'

Always stressing on the importance of I – me – mine. 'Can't get anywhere in this world without a good sense of who you are' – who you are? Who? What? How much? Who you are in the eyes of the world. Who is that? Beginning at the very beginning – I am the connection between the histories of my parents. Of their parents' histories. The history of the world. Born into standard white-gloved hands. Very accustomed to welcoming newborns into the world. Standard procedures. Who was I then? I was cute. As cute as the baby on the Pamper's commercial, as cute as the baby on Nestle's baby food tins. Good thing is was born 1990, not 1977–1977, the year Nestle's baby food was boycotted. Why on earth would anyone want to boycott baby food? Oh yeah, when they were selling it in Africa they ended up accidentally murdering babies, mothers, misinformed on how to use the products, mixed it with infected water, and had no choice – too much pressure from well-meaning white faces

– must not go back to breast feeding – thousands of years of African civilization doesn't know what is best for its babies – Nestle's health nurses gave subsidized supplies of baby milk to hospitals and distributed baby milk samples to African mothers in the hospital.

Good thing I'm me and not them. I started to grow. And grow. And grow. And want. And want. And want. Walking into shops holding my mother's hand I'd point at the Cabbage Patch dolls, Barbies, Lego, and dress-up costumes so that I could be Disney's Sleeping Beauty – she was so perfect, so helpless, so angelic. Who was I? Sleeping Beauty. I would sit for hours playing with Barbie. She was so pretty (of course she was – she was modelled after a German doll called Lilli who was made for sexually frustrated German men to have something pretty to look at, not intended for little German girls). I continued growing. And growing. Stopped wanting to play with Barbie, started wanting to look like Barbie. Didn't want to start inflating in size like the rest of the first world, munching too many chemicals, while starvation problems in the third world don't look any better. But inflation seems inevitable, what with increasingly nothing to do, more to eat. They were selling us boredom through TV sets. So, settled for the inflation, eating my Kit-kats in front of the idiot box that was flashing interchangeably images of mouth-watering McDonalds burgers, starvation in Somalia, and starved supermodels. I wanted the right shoes. Nike. Those were expensive though (so expensive that the people who spend 70 to 80 hours a week making them under gruelling conditions would only be able to afford a pair if they saved up all their pay cheques for three months, and didn't eat, pay rent ...) Of course by the time I started wearing Nike shoes I wasn't eating corporate-made baby food anymore. So what was I eating? These days that's a little hard to tell. The profit-making industries controlling our food supply are shy to share their secrets. Definitely a lot of chemicals. Acids and bases, the kinds of things you mix in science class to give you miniature explosions. Lots of colorings and flavorings (because the things you mix in science class don't taste very good on their own). Possibly genetically modified rice, irradiated beef, hormone-injected chicken (or was it antibiotics?), and pesticide-sprayed fruits and vegetables, possibly not. Corporations don't like to label these things. Apparently forcing them to is a breach of their human rights. Corporations are human now, according to the law, anyway. They are very private 'people' who don't like outsiders butting into their business. Outsiders like you and me. Outsiders who buy what comes out of their mystery factories. They always wrap their goods in such pretty packaging. It's hard to resist.

Resist. Oh, now I'm starting to learn the meaning of resistance. Resist drugs. Resist alcohol. Resist cigarettes. 'Just say no.' They fry your brain, suck your energy, and corrupt you soul. Soul? What soul? Sold it to Hades to cross the river Styx to the underworld and get my quick fix. You go to prison for smoking pot. Well, not really, depends on where you are and what you look like. Here in Lebanon all you need is a rich baba, a prestigious family name, and *wasta*.[1] Otherwise you rot in

1.   'Friends in high places.'

prison. I thought I needed a few more rich connections before I dare to try drugs here in Lebanon, but then it hit me: I'm a woman (cops go easy on women here). I'd be ok in the US if I was blonde, though. Words spoken at a time when Hitler's preference for an Aryan race has supposedly died down – not in some places: 72% of all drug users in the US are white, yet 70% of drug users locked up in prison are black. Prisons are turning out to be fruitful soil for big businesses; they get a large working force practically free of charge. And since criminals are not really human – they have way less rights than their fellow human businesses (it's strange, I wasn't aware that a corporation had more human qualities: emotion, intellect, spirit, soul, magic than a person behind bars …) – no-one cares about them, they might as well work as slaves. But I know that people care about money, so it's surprising that they are willing to spend as much to send a human being to jail as they are to send someone to Harvard – $50,000. Education is so expensive. If you aren't deserving – smart and rich – then you aren't worth the $50,000 education. And also did you know that the privilege to be treated for AIDS is the privilege of the rich? The poor aren't worth it. Health is bought at a high price after we've already spent so much money destroying it. Really destroying it – one in five people in Lebanon have cancer. Probably the same number of people are a cancer to Lebanon.

So if u wants somewhere free from loneliness, expectations, dreams and all the problems I mentioned above – somewhere with warmth and divine love – ignore the world and ourselves in it, delve into the comfort of drugs and turn stone cold and numb. Or we overemphasize our lips with a bit of silicon and hope that that is enough for the world, hope that noone will see beyond it into places we don't dare to explore ourselves. Girls starving themselves to be noticed – dressed in masks with painted faces waiting like Sleeping Beauty waiting for the prince of love to kiss them into an awakening to wonderland. Corporate-owned CNN does not splash across TV screens the ominous threat of terrorism of the spirit ... young people drunk on anti-depressants and ABC shopping malls; high on beauty pageants and heroin; fasting on sugar-free gum diets and, deadliest of all, deficient in caring ...

OVER MY DEAD BODY

John le Carré

Lebanon

So answer me this one, please. If you kill a hundred innocent civilians and one terrorist, are you winning or losing the war on terror? 'Ah,' you may reply, 'but that one terrorist could kill *two* hundred people, a thousand, more!' But then comes another question: if, by killing a hundred innocent people, you are creating five *new* terrorists in the future, and a popular base clamouring to give them aid and comfort, have you achieved a net gain for future generations of your countrymen, or created the enemy you deserve?

On 12th July of this year the Israeli Chief of Staff granted us an insight into the subtleties of his nation's military thinking. The military operations being planned for the Lebanon, he told us, would 'turn back the clock by twenty years'. Well, I was there twenty years ago, and it wasn't a pretty picture. Since then, the General has been as good as his word. I am writing this just twenty-eight days after Hizbullah captured two Israeli soldiers, a common enough military practice not unknown to the Israelis themselves.

In that time, nine hundred and thirty-two Lebanese have been killed and more than three thousand wounded. Nine hundred and thirteen thousand have become refugees. Israel's dead number ninety-four, with eight hundred and sixty-seven wounded. In the first week of this conflict, Hizbullah fired some ninety rockets a day into Israel. Last week – despite eight thousand seven hundred unopposed bombing sorties flown by the Israeli air force, resulting in the crippling of Beirut's international airport, and the destruction of power plants, fuel dumps, fishing fleets, one hundred and forty-seven bridges and seventy-two roads – Hizbullah upped its daily average of rockets to one hundred and sixty-nine. And those two Israeli prisoners who were the purported cause of all the fuss have still not come home.

So yes. Exactly as we were warned, Israel has indeed done to the Lebanon what it did to it twenty years ago: laid waste its infrastructure and visited collective punishment on a delicate, multi-cultural, resilient democracy that was struggling to reconcile its sectarian differences and live in profitable harmony with its neighbours.

Until four weeks ago, Lebanon was being heralded by the United States as a model of what other Middle Eastern countries might become. Hizbullah, it was widely and perhaps optimistically believed by the international community, was loosening its ties with Syria and Iran and on the way to becoming a political rather than a purely military force, yet today this very force is the toast of all Arabia, Israel's reputation for military supremacy is in tatters and its cherished deterrent image no longer deters. And the people of Lebanon have become the latest victims of a global catastrophe that is the work of deluded zealots and has no end in sight.

Tobias Hill

The Wave

In the small hours, the first snow
falls and disappears and falls and

holds to itself,
the ground beneath already sprung with growth.

You bed the blunt new hyacinths in straw
and cut the last hard bud
from the damask rose you planted
last winter by the kitchen door,

and stand there with it in your hand,
out in the dead and buried yard,
as if you are asking yourself
What should I do with this?

How small my writing has become.
All day news of the dead rolls in.

We have observed the silences,
and given. What more can we give?

The death toll mounts every morning.
It grows unspeakable. You wash and dress

by the television's Morse of light,
the volume muted on the silences
which go on here and there around the world
and which, laid end to end, would render us
speechless for life. You check your purse,

keys, travelcard, and look back as you leave
in case you've left the television on,

as if the light that washes our dark room
could still come flooding out. Who would you save
if it did? And look, the flats above the shops
are all awash with that submarine light

that the news brings, and those out on the street
walk fast, as if each of them would escape
something unthinkable. This knowingness.
Nobody knows what else to do with it
but bear it, and it isn't finished yet.

There is much more that we could know,
and nobody can tell where it will stop,

or if it ever will. This is the news.

What should I do with this? you say, and then

What should I do with this?

Nada Awar Jarrar

'There Was No Lebanon
When My Father Was Born'

There was no Lebanon when my father was born. Early in 1918, the mountain region his forefathers had lived in for hundreds of years was still under Ottoman rule. It was not until over two decades later, and after a long period as a French mandate between the wars, that Lebanon became a sovereign nation.

The Lebanon my father knew as a child was a small, predominantly Druze village where pine trees grew in abundance and the snow fell so hard and fast in winter that children were required to take sticks of firewood to school to feed the classroom stove; and come summer, the sun long and hot on their backs, my father and his brothers would run free through the dirt streets of the village then up into the deepening forests where the moon cast its shadow and the wolves called to each other at night.

When he grew older, eventually moving down to Beirut with his family to continue his education, my father experienced a different kind of Lebanon, one that boasted a vibrant city on a glimmering sea, a new world of people and immeasurable possibility, and as his own life expanded to reveal the kind of man he would eventually become, so did Lebanon, slowly emerging as a country that promised to conquer its own future.

At twenty-one, my father made his way to America to spend several years studying at university there. Lebanon became for him then a cherished memory, the only place he longed for in his dreams, a string that pulled at his troubled heart; and in 1943, returning home in the midst of a world war that had already ravaged Europe and changed the Middle East forever, my father discovered a newly independent Lebanon made up of myriad communities that had come together on the strength of hope alone.

By the time he died on July 29, 2006, this country had gone through so much upheaval through self-inflicted violence and savage Israeli wars that, for one moment, I thought that it too had drawn its last breath. Now, wondering in these desperate times where best to direct my grief, I find myself, like my father, harbouring a fierce and protective love for a country that once lived only as a notion in his beautiful mind.

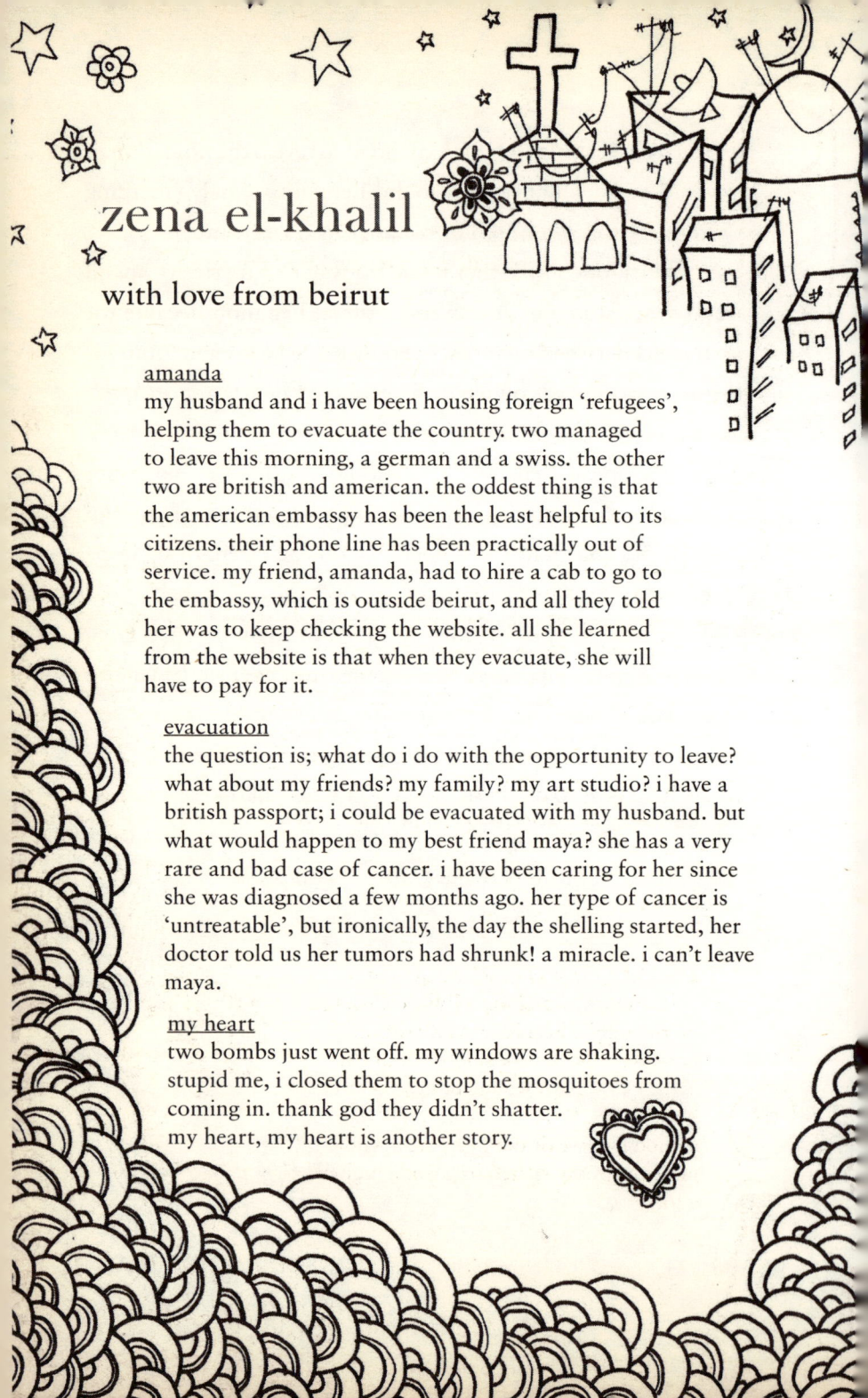

zena el-khalil

with love from beirut

amanda
my husband and i have been housing foreign 'refugees',
helping them to evacuate the country. two managed
to leave this morning, a german and a swiss. the other
two are british and american. the oddest thing is that
the american embassy has been the least helpful to its
citizens. their phone line has been practically out of
service. my friend, amanda, had to hire a cab to go to
the embassy, which is outside beirut, and all they told
her was to keep checking the website. all she learned
from the website is that when they evacuate, she will
have to pay for it.

evacuation
the question is; what do i do with the opportunity to leave?
what about my friends? my family? my art studio? i have a
british passport; i could be evacuated with my husband. but
what would happen to my best friend maya? she has a very
rare and bad case of cancer. i have been caring for her since
she was diagnosed a few months ago. her type of cancer is
'untreatable', but ironically, the day the shelling started, her
doctor told us her tumors had shrunk! a miracle. i can't leave
maya.

my heart
two bombs just went off. my windows are shaking.
stupid me, i closed them to stop the mosquitoes from
coming in. thank god they didn't shatter.
my heart, my heart is another story.

lebanese drivers

today i drove through downtown to visit my parents. i was driving alone and was nervous. i came across a red light and stopped. the streets were empty, and i caught myself wondering why i stopped. then i remembered my latest policy to keep me sane; that even under attack, we should not lose our manners.

i looked into my rearview mirror and saw other cars approaching. i closed my eyes and prayed that they would also stop. that if they didn't cross the light, it would indicate that somehow we are all thinking alike. most of you have heard about lebanese drivers. they never stop at red lights.

ladies and gentlemen, today, they stopped.

bartender

i have no idea what day it is. did the gas blow up yesterday or was it the day before? what does it matter, everything is blowing up.

today a friend told me about a bartender who has not spoken with his family since this whole thing started. he has no idea if they are alive. they have a house in dahiya. he ran there to grab his passport. it is such a huge risk to go anywhere near dahiya. when he got to his home he realized that he would never see his passport again, his building no longer existed. this bartender is stuck in beirut for eternity.

sour

2 weeks ago i was in sour enjoying a cold almaza, watching jellyfish wash up on the public beach. i was there with amanda, who is now safely out of the country. i was showing her how near the border was. little did we know. it was a good day. we drank beer, ate a whole plate of greasy french fries and laughed a lot.

today sour is on fire. today sour is hell on earth. there are still so many people trapped in the city. no way to leave or enter. nor call loved ones. people in the south received calls from a pre-recorded machine demanding that they evacuate. but, when they did, an f16 flew over and blew up a convoy of cars. 20 civilians killed in one blow. mostly women and children.

smell

there is a strong smell in the air. a mixture of burnt buildings, electric fires, and charred bodies. i closed all the windows in the apartment, but now we are choking from this sweltering heat.

maya
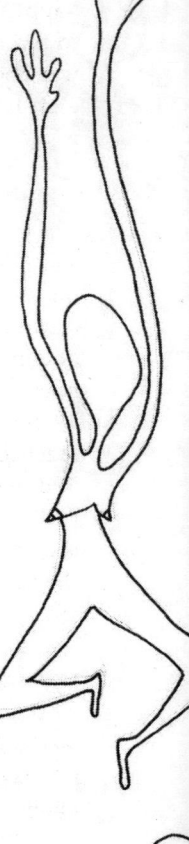

i went to see maya today and she commented on how everyday in beirut is like sunday now. no one on the streets. all the shops closed. but really, it is a lot worse than that. tonight the electricity went out. beirut is so dark and silent.

communication

i noticed that none of us can speak properly any more. we are so tired and drained that it has affected our communication. i am slurring words. i have to repeat myself to get it right. my husband sometimes stops in mid-sentence and zones out. is it related to trauma? fatigue? perhaps despair.

family

i was able to see my family today. we sat on the balcony and talked. it was so dark. so many empty apartments. very few street lights. and so quiet. there is a heavy smog covering beirut from all the bombings.

we spoke politics for a while. everyone
trying to guess what was going to
happen tomorrow and next week, trying
to piece things together. like a game. it
was good to see them.

a friend told me to stock up. i refuse
to stock up. i refuse. i refuse.

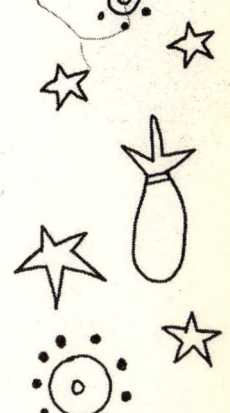

shopping
i finally went to the supermarket. i was
dreading the empty shelves, the people
queuing. what i saw: emptying shelves. long
lines. a priest buying a lot of beer.

there was long-life milk. my hand
reached out for a bottle, and then another,
and then a third. but as i stared into my
trolley, i took one out and put it back on
the shelf, and then the second, and finally
the third. better leave them for a mother's
children.

i bought strange things. things i was
worried i may not find again. i bought
a bottle of triple sec. so that i can make
cosmopolitans for my friends when they
eventually do start coming over to visit
again.

i bought pesto in a jar. i know it will
soon become a luxury item. i bought two
small jars.

i bought sanitary napkins. the ones i like.
i never want to get stuck with those really
thick 1980s bulky ones. i always used to see
them in my cousin's bathroom when we
used to visit beirut in the 80s. they remind
me of war.

i bought smoked almonds. two cans.
i bought more pasta. yuck.

neighbors <1>

my husband keeps walking around the house in
his boxers. i tell him to put some clothes on and
he replies, 'what for? we don't have any neighbors
anymore. they are all gone. who is going to see me?'

hehe. he is right. so i let him off the hook.

neighbors <2>

flyers rained down from the sky. we have deciphered
them as a picture of nasrallah coming out of a
bottle like a genie. he is saying 'any services?'
around him are the presidents of syria, iran, and
hamas. they are all sitting on a map of lebanon.

it's war

people are quickly becoming used to
this. they have stopped going to work
– what's the point? it is war! people
have let go of commitments – what's the
point? it is war! cafes and restaurants
have shut down.

maya: what's wrong with you today?
you look so down … so depressed …
zena, what's wrong? did someone die??
what's wrong???

zena: it's this war.

maya: don't worry. you'll get used to
it. eventually you won't even realize that
there is a war.

zena: i don't think i want to get used
to it.

maya: come on, let's make some
pancakes. it will take your mind off
things. by the way, did i tell you how
much weight you've lost? you look good!

zena: i had been meaning to shed a
few pounds but i didn't think it would
happen like this, and so quickly.

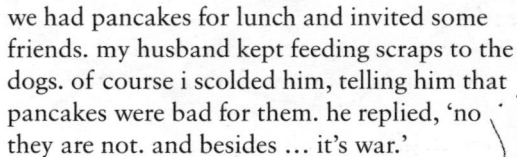

we had pancakes for lunch and invited some
friends. my husband kept feeding scraps to the
dogs. of course i scolded him, telling him that
pancakes were bad for them. he replied, 'no
they are not. and besides … it's war.'

oil

our glorious beaches all covered in black. bays, rocks,
crevices, hidden under a blanket of oil. i cannot explain
how big this spill is. we went as far north as anfe before
turning back. the oil slick continues to travel north, eating up
everything in its path. we heard it has reached syria.
byblos is smothered. the oldest port city on earth, in ruins.
we could smell the oil from miles away. this summer, the
town was celebrating its 7,000th birthday. there were huge
festivities planned. so much effort wasted. now, nothing but
this black plague.

  we stopped to speak with a few fishermen. they are
devastated. they have no means of income anymore. many of
them had fixed up their boats for tourist trips along the coast.

crab

we spotted a crab and he made a dash for it. he
was covered in black oil. totally smothered. the
poor thing. what does he have to do with any of
this?

house of pain

maya is on 5 different painkillers. they make her funny.
whenever i call she answers, 'hello. maya's house of pain. can
i help you.' it's funnier when you hear it on the phone. the sky
is so dark tonight. there is no moon. beirut is quiet. death is all
around me.

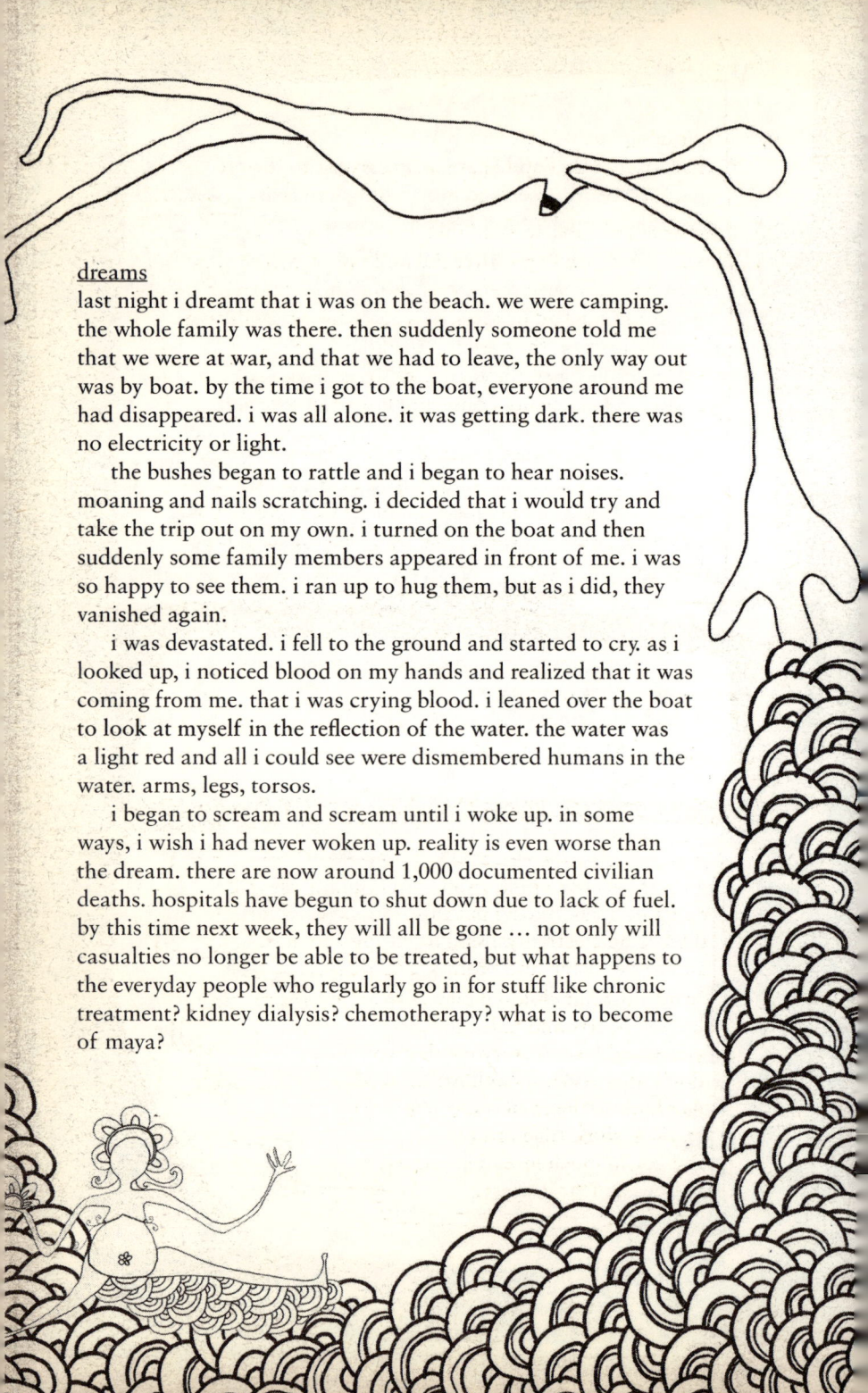

dreams

last night i dreamt that i was on the beach. we were camping. the whole family was there. then suddenly someone told me that we were at war, and that we had to leave, the only way out was by boat. by the time i got to the boat, everyone around me had disappeared. i was all alone. it was getting dark. there was no electricity or light.

the bushes began to rattle and i began to hear noises. moaning and nails scratching. i decided that i would try and take the trip out on my own. i turned on the boat and then suddenly some family members appeared in front of me. i was so happy to see them. i ran up to hug them, but as i did, they vanished again.

i was devastated. i fell to the ground and started to cry. as i looked up, i noticed blood on my hands and realized that it was coming from me. that i was crying blood. i leaned over the boat to look at myself in the reflection of the water. the water was a light red and all i could see were dismembered humans in the water. arms, legs, torsos.

i began to scream and scream until i woke up. in some ways, i wish i had never woken up. reality is even worse than the dream. there are now around 1,000 documented civilian deaths. hospitals have begun to shut down due to lack of fuel. by this time next week, they will all be gone ... not only will casualties no longer be able to be treated, but what happens to the everyday people who regularly go in for stuff like chronic treatment? kidney dialysis? chemotherapy? what is to become of maya?

our house

the last time they were here, they stayed for 18 years.

we were only able to visit my father's village in the south a few years ago, after the pull out. it was the first time i had ever been there. i remember how surreal it was. our home had been used as an army centre during their occupation. they used to detain, interrogate and torture people in our house. after the pull out, we knocked down the old house and built a new one.

we were in that house a little over a month ago for my cousin's birthday. now i don't know if i shall ever see it again. did i tell you my husband and i slept outdoors that night, on the patio? it was so quiet and serene. so peaceful

fuel

in a week, if we do not get fuel into the country, the hospital that maya goes to will be shut down. she will not be able to get her chemotherapy. that is a few days from now.

music

a great friend sent me a song. every time i think I'm going to break down i put this song on full blast. if there is no electricity, i sing it out loud to myself...
and to my sister, and brother, and dogs ...
'why must our children play in the streets,
broken hearts and faded dreams,
peace and love to everyone that you meet,
don't you worry, it could be so sweet,
just look to the rainbow, you will see
sun will shine till eternity,
i've got so much love in my heart,
noone can tear it apart,
yeah,'

feel the love generation,
yeah, yeah, yeah,
    feel the love generation,
c'mon c'mon c'mon c'mon yeah'

on the eve of ceasefire

this morning, i woke up with a smile on my face. my
husband had jumped on top of me, kissing me all over
my face, saying that the war was going to end. that
the un voted. that things were going to get better now.
i had only fallen asleep two hours earlier, but jumped
out of bed with a kind of energy i hadn't had in over a
month. it was a good morning.

    i don't believe that we are born to hate. i believe
that it is conditioned through things like fear, violence,
oppression and misunderstanding.

    life is beautiful. it is a never ending possibility … it
is a first kiss …

    remember that scene in the matrix (the 3rd one),
right at the end, when neo and trinity enter the
machine world … they are flying their plane, holding
hands … love is guiding them through the war zone.
then they shoot up into the sky, cutting away from
the darkness, into the electric clouds … fighting for
their life … then suddenly they get through it and they
see earth for what it really is: clear skies … and then
trinity says 'beautiful.'

    i wonder if we can do that too.

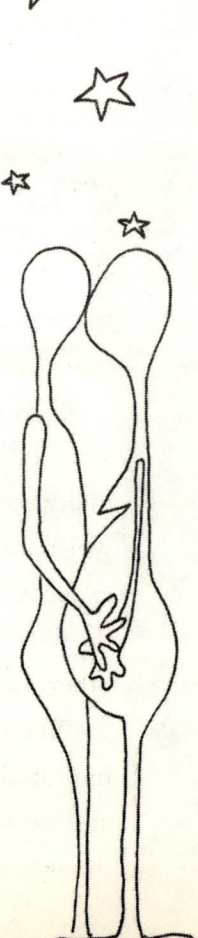

Hanif Kureishi

The Dogs

Overnight it had been raining but to one side of the precipitous stone steps there was a rail to grip onto. With her free hand she took her son's wrist, dragging him back when he lost his footing. It was too perilous for her to pick him up, and at five years old he was too heavy to be carried far.

Branches heavy with sticky leaves trailed across the steps, sometimes blocking their way so they had to climb over or under them. The steps themselves twisted and turned and were worn and often broken. There were more of them than she'd expected. She had never been this way, but had been told it was the only path, and that the man would be waiting for her on the other side of the area.

When they reached the bottom of the steps, her son's mood improved, and he called 'chase me'. This was his favourite game and he set off quickly across the grass, which alarmed her, though she didn't want to scare him with her fears. She pursued him through the narrow wooded area ahead, losing him for a moment. She had to call out for him several times until at last she heard his reply.

Their feet kept sinking into the lush ground but a discernible track emerged. Soon they were in the open. It was a common rather than a park and would take about forty minutes to cross: that was what she had been told.

Though it was a long way off, only a dot in the distance, she noticed the dog right away. Almost immediately the animal seemed bigger, a short-legged compact bullet. She knew all dogs were of different breeds: Dalmatians and chihuahuas and so on, but she had never retained the names. As the dog neared her son she wondered if it wasn't chasing a ball hidden in the grass. But there was no ball that she could see, and the little speeding dog with its studded collar had appeared from nowhere, sprinting across the horizon like a shadow, before turning in their direction. There was no owner in sight; there were no other humans she could see.

The boy saw the dog and stopped, tracking it with curiosity and then with horror. What could his mother do but cry out and begin to run? The dog had already knocked her son down and began not so much to bite him as to eat him, furiously.

She was wearing heavy, loosely laced shoes and was able to give the dog a wild blow in the side, enough to distract it, so that it looked bemused. She pulled the boy to her, but it was impossible for her to examine his wounds because she then had to hold him as high as she could while stumbling along, with the dog still beside her, barking, leaping and twisting in the air.

She could not understand why she had no fascination for the dog.

She began to shout, to scream, panicking because she wouldn't be able to carry her son far. Tiring, she stopped and kicked out at the dog again, this time hitting him in the mouth, which made him lose hope.

Immediately a big long-haired dog was moving in the bushes further away, racing towards them. As it took off to attack the child she was aware, around her, of numerous other dogs, in various colours and sizes, streaming out of the undergrowth from all directions. Who had called them? Why were they there?

She lost her footing, she was pushed over and was huddled on the ground, trying to cover her son, as the animals noisily set upon her, in a ring. To get him they would have to tear through her but it wouldn't take long, there were so many of them, and they were hungry too.

Greta Naufal
Exodus

Adonis

The City

A street whose bowels open with gasps of pain
And the wounds scatter their sons and their sons' sons
To the four winds

I see no idea, no sign
Just a language turned upside down in its own dust

This is indeed a moment
When the soul despairs of its remedies

Dawn, give me your hand now
So I can see the night of talking home

I know for certain: the silence in this city has a voice
And it has the shape of a guitar
And I see the sun as a prayer-mat
Torn to pieces in its hands. And I listen
To the day. The day is an orator
With nothing on his lips but words

Whose sound is strangled.

I know for certain: the silence also has its prophecies

Translated by Catherine Cobham

Mai Ghoussoub

Beirut, a Visible City on the Road

Last week I was sitting through a four-hour train ride from Liverpool to London. In the seats behind me were two young men, one Asian and one West African, both in their early twenties.

They had with them a little gadget broadcasting a very funny Asian sitcom, 'Goodness Gracious me'. I could hear the sketches very clearly, to the point where I decided to put down the book I was reading and start listening. Soon I began really enjoying what I was hearing and forgot all about my book. Suddenly, from a few seats ahead, came a man in his thirties – big, white, very white, almost pink – with a shaved head and a big tattoo covering most of his right shoulder. He started screaming and insulting the two young men.

'Put this … down. Understand me?'

I could see a fight coming.

But to my surprise, the two young men complied immediately. I felt ashamed of myself; I should have interfered. I was offended for them. I was aggressed by the man's rudeness, and I was in no doubt that racism had something to do with his atrocious behaviour. I am telling this story because I still feel ashamed for keeping my words inside my throat. I could at least have told him to ask politely, I could have come to the rescue of these two kids by saying that I was enjoying the sketches too. I didn't, because my space of thinking and acting was restricted by the carriage space. I still feel bad, because I might have been the only one who should have interfered: I understood both the desire of this pink man to defend his individual space and the need of the two young men to share theirs. I am, after all, whatever changes I have witnessed in my life, still from a city, Beirut, a city *par excellence* and moreover a city located on the shores of the Mediterranean, this space/mood that has always known how to include 'the other' and turn it into a 'self'.

I say a city *par excellence* because 'a city is a social community, because it organises itself in a space that assembles its members, because it is inscribed in time and in this sense it is not static even in awareness and representation, because it is made of tensions and divergences, of interactions, of conflicts between its actors.' But a city on the shores of a shared sea is so different from my train carriage, for when things become impossible on land one can always look out, breathe the sea air; the sea opens up to let its inhabitants sail away, or at least dream of reaching other shores.

Beirut! Yes, so different from this train carriage, but somehow similar because of the number of languages that were reaching my ears from the other seats. Beirut – which I have never wanted to become an obsession, a stupid nostalgia that carries with it the lies that are the essence of nostalgia – is still for me what Venice

Beirut persisting memories

represented to Marco Polo. Allow me to borrow shamelessly from Italo Calvino's wonderful *Invisible Cities*:

> 'Sir,' says Marco Polo to Kublai Khan, 'Now I have told you about the cities I know.'
>
> 'There is still one city of which you never speak.'
>
> Marco Polo bowed his head.
>
> 'Venice,' the Khan said.
>
> Marco smiled: 'What else do you think I have been telling you about?'

The emperor did not turn a hair. 'And yet I have never heard you mention that name.'

And Polo said 'Every time I describe a city I am saying something about Venice.'

This is why, every time I describe a city, or visit one, I am describing Beirut and revisiting it.

This is not an homage, not a celebration of a city; far from it. For, unfortunately, I also owe this city for familiarizing me with the injustices and corruption that one encounters, to a greater or lesser degree, throughout the cities of the world. Let's call it a *recognition*, a fact that I did not appreciate enough when I first settled in London, away from the Mediterranean, that open promise that had gently caressed my adolescence before throwing me, through fire and blood, from its shores. It threw me towards a city polar opposite to the one I grew up in, an Anglo-Saxon city to the core, a city that lived inside, in dim light, with no shore and no café life. Beirut is a city *al fresco*, very conspicuous thanks to its loud fun, to its noisy joys, but also to the thunderous rumbling of its violent outbreaks. My lucidity is unfortunately indebted to both these opposites. Without Beirut, the city of the south, without its life in translation, I would never have been capable of surviving happily in the cities of the north. It is thanks to my background that I felt that my duty was not only to integrate positively into another urban space, but also and mainly to feel unashamed about dreaming of influencing, of making an impact on 'the other', on the shifting identities of 'the desirable' urban spaces, the metropolises of today.

Background! I love this word, so much more desirable than the word 'identity', or 'root'. Identity and root presume a settled or pure essence; they thrive in times of trouble, often preceding them. Background is synonymous with base, it is located somewhere *behind*, a reality one can refer to, but which can be ignored or abandoned. Our background is not exactly our root; it is the soil in which many realities can grow, but where others can be planted as well.

'A carrot is a root' says my friend to her husband, who keeps nagging her about returning to his country, to his roots. 'I am not a carrot,' she keeps screaming back at him.

Beirut was, is, a city that travels in many directions. Let's look at its calligraphy: it moves and reads in many directions, right to left, left to right, and, yes, for a long time now from top to bottom or bottom to top. I am speaking of the multitude of signs and adverts and billboard invitations to consume that coloured my trips to school for many years and that still fascinate me whenever I walk the city. When you read in opposite directions you're not impermeable to other readings. Maybe this is why, when, during the civil war, my colleague André Gaspard and I landed in Britain, knowing almost nobody there, we felt unselfconscious about the difficulties of starting a bookshop and publishing house, and functioning in what was our third language, English.

I'll tell you an embarrassing story: when we opened our bookshop we needed addresses for our catalogue mailing list. This was 1979; we were newly arrived in England. We went through the telephone directory for nights on end looking for potential customers, through the listings, looking for the al-something, or the Oriental this or that … I'm afraid many of our catalogues may have landed in Chinese restaurants or Thai sex shops. We were a bit lost, but no doubt keen. I sometimes think that this naïve optimism is inherited from my great grandfather, who, fleeing another war, the first big one, jumped on a boat, paying the fee to the captain to take him to America. The captain threw my great-grandfather, as well as many of his co-villagers, onto the shores of the French Guinea. 'You are in America,' he said to them. This is why they called Africa 'America' in my grandfather's village for years afterwards. Meanwhile in Africa, my great-grandfather made a decent living and sent money to educate his children, who acquired, hopefully, a better knowledge of geography.

If I hadn't been brought up in a city that wrote in opposite directions I wouldn't have been able to survive and enjoy the London of today, with its multi-ethnic, fusion culture and juxtaposed realities. Beirut, with its words moving in different directions, made me sceptical, very early on, of the word 'truth', and of the now-unfortunately fashionable labels of 'evil' and 'good'. It was in my *Lycée Francais de Beirut* that the Crusaders were either saints or cruel colonisers, depending on whether the textbooks were in French, from left to right, or in Arabic, from right to left. These opposite but co-existent readings warned me that truth can be perceived differently according to one's location in terms of history, geography and, most importantly, aspiration. This is why I found myself sitting on the train refusing to accept this little fight over space as a so-called 'clash of cultures' or worse, a 'clash of civilisations'.

But it was also because in Beirut I had read Simone de Beauvoir in French, Abu Nuwas in Arabic and Margaret Mead at the American University of Beirut, that I could face this old male chauvinist English banker who kept asking for my boss when I came to open an account for Saqi Books. This was a long time ago – some twenty-five years – and male chauvinism has witnessed a few defeats since then in Britain. But this tweed-jacketed dignified man did not find it undignified to keep asking me, as if he was hard of hearing, to 'let your boss come and sign for the account'. I kept telling him, 'But I am also a director,' what he calls 'a boss', but to no avail. I moved from his bank to another without wasting much time, and lived happily ever after.

It is because I walked from Achrafieh to Ras Beirut, via Ain al-Rumaneh or al-Bourj, by houses that offered their modest balconies to my eyes or their imposing high-rise glass facades, as well as their oriental late-Ottoman arcades that I feel at home in New York as well as in Fez. I walked the same route all through my early twenties, humming the tunes of Edith Piaf, Um Kulsum and Feyrouz, as well as John Coltrane and the Rolling Stones, so that when I reached other cities, *any* other city, I could sing and dance to the same rhythms of those who were already there.

I went to another city, and it became mine, I became proud of some of its monuments and customs: London is home as well. London, so different, but also a space that generously lives out its co-existing realities today. Let me quote from *Invisible Cities* once more:

'In Mauralia', says Marco Polo to Kublai Khan, 'the traveller is invited to visit the city and at the same time, to examine some old postcards that show it as it used to be: The same identical square with a hen in the place of the bus station, a bandstand in the place of the overpass, two young ladies with a parasol in the place of the munitions factory. If the traveller does not wish to disappoint the inhabitants he must praise the postcard city and prefer it to the present one ... It is pointless to ask whether the new ones (cities) are better than the old, since there is no connection between them, just as the old postcards do not depict Mauralia as it was, but a different city which, by chance, was called Mauralia, like this one.'

I hope I did not describe my city as it is portrayed in the postcards, for I am not one for nostalgia, and I thank Beirut for having prepared me to see migration as a promise of adventure. I have to say that only London – the London of today, not that of Victorian postcards – has given me the chance to live in a multiracial environment, where the Asian is the computer engineer who enhances my capacity to access the net, as well as the newsagent next door or the student in my evening class, while my other city, Beirut today, gives me one image, a unique and narrow one of an Asian: an oppressed, over-exploited immigrant housemaid.

Let me tell you about my latest experience in London. Over the last three years I've been exploring the theme of prejudice through appearance and dress code. In 'Dressing-Re-addressing', an installation that dressed people on book covers or cinema posters in the outfits of 'the other', I have been observing the reaction of 'locals' to the shift in external appearance. In London and Vancouver, the symbols were 'orientalised', while in Beirut they were 'occidentalised'.

A few months ago I pushed the exploration further: I dressed as a veiled Lolita, sucking the pipe of a narghile instead of a lollipop; I wore the long robe of Lawrence of Arabia; and a Muslim woman's white tennis outfit, covering my whole body except for my eyes. The latter outfit was purchased in Egypt, in an Islamic sports shop for women. I walked the streets of East London in all of these costumes, carrying my tennis racquet, or sucking my lollipop through my veil, and waited to see how people would respond. Nothing: the Londoners turned their gaze immediately away! They didn't see me! They don't interfere! They saw but made sure they had not looked. I admit that I am still puzzled by this over-tolerant attitude. If I had done the same in Paris, I would have at least heard the familiar '*Rentrez chez vous*'. In Beirut, I am sure, a crowd of kids would have pointed their fingers at me and most probably followed me around.

I hope that soon I'll take my performance and my artistic exploration of 'prejudice' to as many cities as possible.

I hope my city, Beirut, is relearning to be a true cosmopolitan space, a cosmopolitan space in the age of global reality, where the 'others' are, again, also 'us' and where juxtaposition is fighting hierarchy.

Once more from Calvino before I go:

The question that now begins to gnaw at your mind is more anguished: outside Penthesilia does an outside exist? Or, no matter how far you go from the city, will you only pass from one limbo to another, never managing to leave it?

George Szirtes

Clear

> *... It is not your system or clear sight that mills*
> *Down to the consequence a life requires*
> (William Empson)

To be clear about all this, to be clear at all,
is a disgrace not a virtue, I tell
myself, here where I hear no bombs fall,
where all is – relatively speaking – well.

To be clear is to be convinced about things
like death, the concept of justice,
and the necessity of certain actions. But day brings
no solutions nor does devoted practice

make anything perfect. Perfection is the light
in its socket, the sound of the car
cruising down the lane, the burst and flight
of the swift overhead, the ever distant star

above the roof. And this is as perfect and just
as things go, as perfect an operation
as anyone manages in the noise and dust
of any possibility, including annihilation.

So says the child to the hole in the ceiling
if it could but say it, to the tongue
that bursts into light, to the lost feeling
in its limbs, to the debris in the lung.

The only clear thing in history is pain.
The only clear thing in history is silence.
In suffering there is no equality. In the hot rain
of silence there is no balance.

V. S. Naipaul

The Mourners

I walked up the back stairs into the veranda white in the afternoon sun. I could never bring myself to enter that house by the front stairs. We were poor relations; we had been taught to respect the house and the family.

On the right of the veranda was the kitchen, tiled and spruce and with every modern gadget. An ugly Indian girl with a pockmarked face and slack breasts was washing some dishes. She wore a dirty red print frock.

When she saw me she said, 'Hello, Romesh.' She had opened brightly but ended on a subdued tone that was more suitable.

'Hello,' I said softly. 'Is she there?' I jerked my thumb towards the drawing-room that lay straight ahead.

'Yes. Boy, she cries all day. And the baby was so cute too.' The servant girl was adapting herself to the language of the house.

'Can I go in now?'

'Yes,' she whispered. Drying her hands on her frock, she led the way. Her kitchen was clean and pure, but all the impurities seemed to have stuck on her. She tiptoed to the jalousied door, opened it an inch or two, peered in deferentially and said in a louder voice, 'Romesh here, Miss Sheila.'

There was a sigh inside. The girl opened the door and shut it behind me. The curtains had been drawn all around. The room was full of a hot darkness smelling of ammonia and oil. Through the ventilation slits some light came into the room, enough to make Sheila distinct. She was in a loose lemon housecoat; she half sat, half reclined on a pink sofa.

I walked across the polished floor as slowly and silently as I could. I shifted my eyes from Sheila to the table next to the sofa. I didn't know how to begin.

It was Sheila who broke the silence. She looked me up and down in the half-light and said, 'My, Romesh, you are growing up.' She smiled with tears in her eyes. 'How are you? And your mother?'

Sheila didn't like my mother. 'They're all well – all at home are well,' I said. 'And how are you?'

She managed a little laugh. 'Still *living*. Pull up a chair. No, no – not yet. Let me look at you. My, you are getting to be a handsome young man.

I pulled up a chair and sat down. I sat with my legs wide apart at first. But this struck me as being irreverent and too casual. So I put my knees together and let my hands rest loosely on them. I sat upright. Then I looked at Sheila. She smiled.

Then she began to cry. She reached for the damp handkerchief on the table. I got up and asked whether she would like the smelling salts or the bay rum. Jerking with sobs, she shook her head and told me, in words truncated by tears, to sit down.

I sat still, not knowing what to do.

With the handkerchief she wiped her eyes, pulled out a larger handkerchief from her housecoat and blew her nose. Then she smiled. 'You must forgive me for breaking down like this,' she said.

I was going to say, 'That's all right,' but the words felt too free. So I opened my mouth and made an unintelligible noise.

'You never knew my son, Romesh?'

'I only saw him once,' I lied; and instantly regretted the lie. Suppose she asked me where I had seen him or when I had seen him. In fact, I never knew that Sheila's baby was a boy until he died and the news spread.

But she wasn't going to examine me. 'I have some pictures of him.' She called in a gentle, strained voice: 'Soomintra.'

The servant girl opened the door. 'You want something, Miss Sheila?'

'Yes, Soomin,' Sheila said (and I noticed that she had shortened the girl's name, a thing that was ordinarily not done). 'Yes, I want the snapshots of Ravi.' At the name she almost burst into tears, but flung her head back at the last moment and smiled.

When Soomintra left the room I looked at the walls. In the dim light I could make out an engraving of the Princes in the Tower, a print of a stream lazing bluely beautiful through banks cushioned with flowers. I was looking at the walls to escape looking at Sheila. But her eyes followed mine and rested on the Princes in the Tower.

'You know the story?' she asked.

'Yes.'

'Look at them. They're going to be killed, you know. It's only in the past two days I've really got to understand that picture, you know. The boys. So sad. And look at the dog. Not understanding a thing. Just wanting to get out.'

'It is a sad picture.'

She brushed a tear from her eye and smiled once more. 'But tell me, Romesh, how are you getting on with your studies?'

'As usual.'

'Are you going away?'

'If I do well in the exams.'

'But you're bound to do well. After all, your father is no fool.'

It seemed overbearingly selfish to continue listening. I said, 'You needn't talk, if you don't want to.'

Soomintra brought the snapshot album. It was an expensive album, covered in leather. Ravi had been constantly photographed from the time he had been allowed into the open air to the month before his death. There were pictures of him in bathing costume, digging sand on the east coast, the north coast and the south coast; pictures of Ravi dressed up for Carnival, dressed up for tea parties; Ravi on tricycles, Ravi in motor cars, real ones and toy ones; Ravi in the company of scores of people I didn't know. I turned the pages with due lassitude. From time to time Sheila leaned forward and commented. 'There's Ravi at the home of that American doctor. A wunnerful guy. He looks sweet, doesn't he? And look at this one: that boy always had a smile for the camera. He always knew what we were doing. He was a very smart little kid.'

At last we exhausted the snapshots. Sheila had grown silent towards the end. I felt she had been through the album many times in the past two days.

I tapped my hands on my knees. I looked at the clock on the wall and the Princes in the Tower. Sheila came to the rescue. 'I am sure you are hungry.'

I shook my head faintly.

'Soomin will fix something for you.'

Soomintra did prepare something for me, and I ate in the kitchen – their food was always good. I prepared to face the farewell tears and smiles. But just then the Doctor came. He was Sheila's husband and everyone knew him as 'The Doctor'. He was tall with a pale handsome face that now looked drawn and tired.

'Hello, Romesh.'

'Hello, Doctor.'

'How is she?'

'Not very happy.'

'She'll be all right in a couple of days. The shock, you know. And she's a very delicate girl.'

'I hope she gets over it soon.'

He smiled and patted me on the shoulder. He pulled the blinds to shut out the sun from the veranda, and made me sit down.

'You knew my son?'

'Only slightly.'

'He was a fine child. We wanted – or rather, I wanted – to

enter him in the Cow and Gate Baby Contest. But Sheila didn't care for the idea.'

I could find nothing to say.

'When he was four he used to sing, you know. All sorts of songs. In English and Hindi. You know that song – *I'll Be Seeing You*?'

I nodded.

'He used to sing that through and through. He had picked up all the words. Where from I don't know, but he'd picked them up. And even now I don't know half the words myself. He was like that. Quick. And do you know the last words he said to me were "I'll be seeing you in all the old familiar places"? When Sheila heard that he was dead she looked at me and began to cry. "I'll be seeing you," she said.'

I didn't look at him.

'It makes you think, doesn't it? Makes you think about life. Here today. Gone tomorrow. It makes you think about life and death, doesn't it? But here I go, philosophizing again. Why don't you start giving lessons to children?' he asked me abruptly. 'You could make tons of money that way. I know a boy who's making fifty dollars a month by giving lessons one afternoon a week.'

'I am busy with my exams.'

He paid no attention. 'Tell me, have you seen the pictures we took of Ravi last Carnival?'

I hadn't the heart to say yes.

'Soomin,' he called, 'bring the photograph album.'

Hanan al-Shaykh

No

'No,' screamed the little girl as her mother lifted her from her bed, 'I want to stay here till morning. How else would the tooth fairy find me?'

'No,' cried her pillow as the girl left it, 'I need her warmth.'

'No,' whispered her grandfather as she started to disappear into the terrorized crowds, 'I want to see her biting into her apple and singing.'

'No,' pleaded the mother as she held her daughter, 'I want to run away with her. If only I could return her to the safety of my womb.'

'No,' prayed her brother, 'it is too early for me to die. Can I not grow just a little older?'

'No,' lamented their house, 'I did not mean to turn memories into dust.'

'No,' shouted another house, 'I did not want to collapse over those whom I love.'

'No,' protested the empty streets, 'we do not want to suffer the silence of the absent.'

'No,' bellowed the heart of the city, 'I do not want to hear the hooting of the owls.'

'No,' roared the earth, 'I do not want the tanks to wrench my guts.'

'No,' howled Beirut, 'I do not want the sea to cry again.'

'No,' wailed the South, 'I still want to trace my face on my country's map.'

'No,' implored History, 'I do not want to be a parrot with no memory.'

'No,' said Life, 'I do not want to abandon this little girl.'

'No,' sighed the tooth fairy, 'I do not want the little girl's tooth to turn to fire.'

'No,' begged War, 'I do not want to be well again.'

Translated by Amal Ghandour

Yann Martel

Fear

I must say a word about fear. It is life's only true opponent. Only fear can defeat life. It is a clever, treacherous adversary, how well I know. It has no decency, respects no law or convention, shows no mercy. It goes for your weakest spot, which it finds with unerring ease. It begins in your mind, always. One moment you are feeling calm, self-possessed, happy. Then fear, disguised in the garb of mild-mannered doubt, slips into your mind like a spy. Doubt meets disbelief and disbelief tries to push it out. But disbelief is a poorly armed foot soldier. Doubt does away with it with little trouble. You become anxious. Reason comes to do battle for you. You are reassured. Reason is fully equipped with the latest weapons technology. But, to your amazement, despite superior tactics and a number of undeniable victories, reason is laid low. You feel yourself weakening, wavering. Your anxiety becomes dread.

Fear next turns fully to your body, which is already aware that something terribly wrong is going on. Already your lungs have flown away like a bird and your guts have slithered away like a snake. Now your tongue drops dead like an opossum, while your jaw begins to gallop on the spot. Your ears go deaf. Your muscles begin to shiver as if they had malaria and your knees to shake as though they were dancing. Your heart strains too hard, while your sphincter relaxes too much. And so with the rest of your body. Every part of you, in the manner most suited to it, falls apart. Only your eyes work well. They always pay proper attention to fear.

Quickly you make rash decisions. You dismiss your last allies: hope and trust. There, you've defeated yourself. Fear, which is but an impression, has triumphed over you.

The matter is difficult to put into words. For fear, real fear, such as shakes you to your foundation, such as you feel when you are brought face to face with your mortal end, nestles in your memory like a gangrene: it seeks to rot everything, even the words with which to speak of it. So you must fight hard to express it. You must fight hard to shine the light of words upon it. Because if you don't, if your fear becomes a wordless darkness that you avoid, perhaps even manage to forget, you open yourself to further attacks of fear because you never truly fought the opponent who defeated you.

Judith Kazantzis

The Refugee

'I saw Umm Taha
on my way to the village courtyard.
She cried and said,
"You better go and see
your dead husband."
I found him.
He was shot in the back of the head.
I pulled him to the shade.
I couldn't dig a grave for him.

Umm Hussein and I
carried him
on a piece of wood to the cemetery.
I buried him sideways in his mother's grave.
… Until today I worry and pray
that I buried him in the right way,
in the proper position.

I stayed in Kabri
which was the name of my village
for six days without eating anything.
Then I fled into Syria.'

*This 'found poem' is taken verbatim from the English translation
of a UN witness statement.*

Robert Fisk

One Week in the Life and Death of Beirut

Sunday 16 July

It is the first time I have actually seen a missile in this war. They fly too fast – or you are too busy trying to run away to look for them – but this morning, Abed and I actually see one pierce the smoke above us. 'Habibi (my friend)!' he cries, and I start screaming 'Turn the car round, turn it round,' and we drive away for our lives from the southern suburbs. As we turn the corner there is a shattering explosion and a mountain of grey smoke blossoming from the road we have just left. What happened to the men and women we saw running for their lives from that Israeli rocket? We do not know. In air raids, all you see is the few square yards around you. You get out and you survive and that is enough.

I go home to my apartment on the Corniche and find that the electricity is cut. Soon, no doubt, the water will be cut. But I sit on my balcony and reflect that I am not crammed into a filthy hotel in Kandahar or Basra but living in my own home and waking each morning in my own bed. Power cuts and fear and the lack of petrol now that Israel is bombing gas stations mean that the canyon of traffic which honks and roars outside my home until two in the morning has gone. When I wake in the night, I hear the birds and the wash of the Mediterranean and the gentle brushing of palm leaves.

I went to buy groceries this evening. There is no more milk but plenty of water and bread and cheese and fish. When Abed pulls up to let me out of the car, the man in the 4x4 behind us puts his hand permanently on the horn, and when I get out of Abed's car, he mouths the words '*kiss ukhtak*' at me. 'Fuck your sister.' It is the first time I have been cursed in this war. The Lebanese do not normally swear at foreigners. They are a polite people. I hold my hand out, palm down and twist it palm upwards in the Lebanese manner, meaning 'what's the problem?' But he drives away. Anyway, I don't have a sister.

Monday 17 July

The phones are still working and my mobile chirrups like a budgerigar. Too many of the calls are from friends who want to know if they should flee Beirut or flee Lebanon, or from Lebanese who are outside Lebanon and want to know if they should return. I can hear the bombs rumbling across Hizbullah's area of the southern suburbs but I cannot answer these questions. If I advise friends to stay and they are killed, I am responsible. If I tell them to leave and they are killed in their cars, I am responsible. If I tell them to come back and they die, I am responsible. So I tell them how dangerous Lebanon has become and tell them it is their decision. But I feel great sorrow for them. Many have been refugees four times in twenty-four years. Today I am called by a Lebanese woman with Lebanese and Iranian citizenship and one child with a US passport and another with only a Lebanese passport. Her situation is hopeless. I suggest she travels to the Christian mountains around Faraya and try to find a chalet. It will be safe there. I hope.

I come back from Kfar Chim where part of an Israeli missile or an aircraft wing has just partially decapitated the driver of a car. He looked so tragic, his head lolling forward in the driver's seat, just looking at all the blood splashing down his body on to the floor. Abed was getting spooked because I spent too long at the scene. The Israelis always come back. 'Habibi, you took too long. Never stay that long again!' He is right. The Israelis did come back and bombed the Lebanese army.

Now my housemaid Fidele is spooked. She thinks it is too dangerous to travel from the Christian district of Beirut to my home since the Israelis blew the top off the local lighthouse 400 metres from my front door. Fidele is from Togo and makes fantastic pizzas (I recommend her Pizza Togolaisi to anyone) so I send Abed off to pick her up and bring her to my home for one hour. She puts my dirty clothes in the washing machine, and after five minutes the power goes off and we have to take them all out and try again tomorrow.

Tuesday 18 July
At 3.45am I wake to the sound of tank tracks and a big military motor heaving away in the darkness. I go downstairs to find that the Lebanese army has positioned an American-made armoured personnel carrier in the car park opposite my home.

It has been placed strategically under some palm trees, as if this will stop Israeli aircraft from spotting it. I don't like this at all and nor does my landlord, Mustafa, who lives downstairs. The Lebanese army is now an occasional target for the Israelis and this little behemoth looks like a palm tree disguised as a tank. Later in the morning, I call a general in the army who is a friend of mine and army operations calls me back to check the location. It takes an hour before they find the car park on their maps. Then I receive another call telling me that the APC is next to my home to prevent the Hizbullah from using the car park to launch another missile at an Israeli ship. The empty American Community School is just up my road. The Lebanese army is defending us.

The first French warship arrives to pick up French citizens fleeing Lebanon. It steams proudly past my balcony. Many French naval vessels are named after great military leaders, and this particular anti-submarine frigate is called the *Jean-de-Vienne*. I pad off to consult my little library of French history books. Jean de Vienne, it turns out, was a fourteenth-century French admiral who raided the Sussex town of Rye and the Isle of Wight and who was killed – oh lordy, lordy – fighting in the Crusades against the Muslim Turks. A suitable ship to start France's evacuation of the ancient Crusader port of Beirut.

Wednesday 19 July
Now that the Israelis are destroying whole apartment blocks in the Shia southern suburbs – there is a permanent umbrella of smoke over the seafront, stretching far out into the

Mediterranean – tens of thousands of Shia Muslims have come to seek sanctuary in the undamaged part of Beirut, in the parks and schools and beside the sea. They walk back and forth outside my home, the women in chadors, their bearded husbands and brothers silently looking at the sea, their children playing happily around the palm trees. They speak to me with anger about Israel but choose not to discuss the depth of cynicism of the Shia Hizbullah who provoked Israel's brutality by capturing two of its soldiers. As well as the Hizbullah, the Israelis are now targeting food factories and trucks and buses – not to mention 46 bridges – and the bin men are now reluctant to pick up the rubbish skips each night for fear their innocent rubbish truck is mistaken for a missile launcher. So no rubbish collection this morning.

The local Beirut papers are filled with photographs that would never be seen in the pages of a British paper: of decapitated babies and women with no legs or arms or of old men in bits. Israel's air raids are promiscuous and – when you see the results as we now do with our own eyes – obscene. No doubt Hizbullah's equally innocent civilian victims in Israel look like this but the slaughter in Lebanon is on an infinitely more terrible scale. The Lebanese look at these pictures and see them on television – as does the rest of the Arab world – and I wonder how many of them are provoked to think of another 9/11 or 7/7 or whatever the next date will be.

What does war do to people? Later, I am talking to an Austrian journalist and idly ask what her father does. 'He drinks,' she says. Why? 'Because his father was killed at Stalingrad.'

I walk across with tea for the soldiers on the APC in the car park. They are all from Baalbek, Shia Muslims. They would never open fire on a Hizbullah missile crew. Then I return home from another visit to the southern suburbs and find they have gone, along with their behemoth. The first good news of the day.

The minister of finance holds a press conference to talk of the billions of dollars of damage being done to Lebanon by Israel's air raids. 'We have had pledges of aid from Saudi Arabia, Kuwait and Qatar,' he proudly announces. 'And from Syria and Iran?' the man from Irish radio asks, naming Hizbullah's two principal supporters in the Muslim world. 'Nothing,' the minister replies dismissively.

Thursday 20 July

A bad day for messages. Phone calls from the States to tell me I am an anti-Semite for criticising Israel. Here we go again. To call decent folk anti-Semites is soon going to make anti-Semitism respectable, I tell the callers before asking them to tell the Israeli air force to stop killing civilians. Then a fax from a Jewish friend in California to tell me that a man called Lee Kaplan – 'a columnist for the Israel National News', whatever that is – has condemned me in print for developing a 'high-paid speaking career among anti-Semites'. Unlike Benjamin Netanyahu and many others I can think of, I never take money for lecturing – ever – but to smear the thousands of ordinary Americans who listen to me as anti-Semites is outrageous.

Another fax from the editor of the forthcoming paperback

edition of my book, apologising for bothering me at a 'very difficult (sic) time' but promising to send me page proofs by DHL which is still operating to Beirut. I go downtown to check this with DHL. Yes, the man says, parcels for Lebanon are sent to Jordan and then in a truck via Damascus to Beirut. A truck, I say to myself. Ouch.

Friday 21 July
The Israelis have just bombed Khiam prison. An interesting target since this was the jail in which Israel's former proxy militia, the South Lebanon Army, used to torture male prisoners by attaching electrodes to their penises and female prisoners by electrocuting their breasts. When the Israeli army retreated in 2000, the Hizbullah turned the prison into a museum. Now the evidence of the SLA's cruelty has been erased. Another 'terrorist' target.

The power comes back at home at 11pm and I watch Israel's consul general, Arye Mekel, telling the BBC that Israel is 'doing the Lebanese a favour' by bombing Hizbullah, insisting that 'most Lebanese appreciate what we are doing'. So now I understand. The Lebanese must thank the Israelis for destroying their lives and infrastructure. They must be grateful for all the air strikes and the dead children. It's as if the Hizbullah claimed that Israelis should be grateful to them for attacking Zionism. How far can self-delusion reach?

Saturday 22 July
I have coffee in my landlord's garden and he climbs an old

wooden ladder into his fig tree and brings me a plate of fruit. 'Every day it gives us our figs,' he tells me. 'We sit under our tree in the afternoon and with the breeze off the sea, it is like air conditioning.' I look at his little paradise of pot plants and sip my Arabic coffee from a little blue mug. We watch the warships sliding into Beirut port. 'What will happen when all the foreigners have gone?' he asks. That's what we are all asking. We shall find out this week.

Ali Smith

An End to Sleep

Take the eye of my child, here, take it.
Does that make you worth more?

Here's my right arm, go on, break it.
Does that make you worth more?

You can humiliate me, naked.
Does that make you worth more?

Give me your sleeping child. I'll wake it.
I'll smash its head on my door.

Does that make me worth more?

Raymond Briggs

Bomber 1944

An insurance clerk
of twenty two
now a bomber pilot
became fixated
by his foot

He found that if
he tensed his foot
slightly
during the final bomb run
the rudder would move
slightly
and the bomber would drift
slightly
to the left or to the right
so slightly
even his bomb aimer
would be unaware

Bombs gone!

A ton of bombs
then fell
on slightly different streets
on slightly different houses
and different people
would be killed

raid after raid
night after night
week after week
ton upon ton of bombs

hundreds of people
selected to live or to die
by the slight tension
of his foot

the slight tension
of his foot
caused a greater tension
in his mind

the insurance clerk
now twenty three
suffered a breakdown
was taken off bombers
and once again
became a clerk.

Jean Said Makdisi

The Little Girl with Gold Earrings

In the midst of all the horrors, it was the picture of a little girl with gold earrings that especially got to me. She was lying there, on the floor of her house, alongside her brothers and sisters and her mother, all of them covered with bloodstained shrouds.

Perhaps that little girl entered my heart so directly and vividly because when she died in the early days of the current war, my husband and I were looking after our two little granddaughters in the absence of their parents, who were away on a short trip. It was my special role to wipe away their every tear, and kiss every little bump and cut, to hold their precious little bodies close to mine as I read them a story and prepared them for bed every night. When I saw that little girl's picture, I felt that if I had picked her up she would have felt just the same as my little granddaughters did, warm and soft. Before she smelt of blood and death, she would have smelt sweet after her bath, as they did. And if I had stroked her face, or combed her hair, now all tangled and matted with blood, she would have laughed or cried the same way my granddaughters did. But she was dead, terribly and irrevocably dead, and I could not bear the cruelty of it.

My son and his wife had left before the war began and were now frantic to get home to their daughters. The morning they were to make their perilous journey home, my husband and I sat watching the children play in the garden, not voicing our fears to one another. Suddenly, we heard the scream of jets overhead, and then two loud explosions. I froze. My husband leapt to his feet and went to the radio. He returned a few minutes later, his face ashen. The Israelis had bombed the road they were on. We sat there, silent, passive, knowing there was nothing we could do, no way to find out if they were alive or dead, or left to die in a burning car, screaming for help, as so many others had in the last few days.

An hour passed. A car drove up. I saw my son, and his wife. I never wept as I wept then. Later, they told us they had passed a convoy carrying emergency medical supplies, including several ambulances. It had been bombed only a few minutes after they passed it.

Our story had a happy ending. Not so the hundreds of thousands who have been made homeless, or the hundreds, many of them children, who have been killed in the air-raids, not only in Lebanon, but in Palestine as well. I have seen dead children pulled out of the rubble of their homes; I have seen children weeping over the bodies of their dead mothers and fathers, and parents weeping over the bodies of their dead children. I have seen dismembered children, decapitated children, burned children, mutilated children. Terrified children, screaming. I have seen little faces pockmarked with shrapnel wounds, their beauty ruined forever.

But somehow my heart always turns to the little girl with the earrings. Perhaps her grandmother had lovingly given them to her with a big hug and kiss, as I had so often kissed and hugged my little grandchildren. Perhaps that connection, made from my own memory and experience, is why I feel I knew her well, though I never met her or said her name. Perhaps that is why I am so haunted by the picture of her lying dead, wrapped in that bloodstained shroud.

We have been told by the unspeakably cruel Messrs. Bush and Blair, and the well-dressed Condoleeza Rice, that the deaths of this little girl, the children of Qana, and all the other innocents, are aspects of legitimate Israeli self-defense. Though they issue pious statements regretting the 'tragic loss of innocent lives', they say they are determined to continue 'their struggle against evil', gallantly 'staying the course', and that there will be no ceasefire until 'the job is done'.

That these people use the language of morality to justify and support Israeli war crimes, not only in Lebanon but also in Palestine, where they have granted active support for decades of unimaginably vicious military occupation, adds to their complicity in murder and mayhem throughout the world. Resistance to their inhumanity and their hypocrisy can only lie in the urgent demand of good people throughout the world that the Israeli war machine, which cannot operate without American support, be bridled at once. Only then will the terrible suffering of the people of this region, and the unforgivable slaughter of children such as my little girl with the gold earrings, end.

THE CROSS WAS A CLEAR TARGET

Kamila Shamsie

Miscarriage

Mrs Shaukut, owner of scratched records, would have been the mother of both a son and a daughter if her second-born, fingers perfectly formed, had not been a pickled specimen in a hospital less than a mile away. In the early morning, Mrs Shaukut tracked footprints around her dew-drenched garden and waited to hear cries from fragile lungs. Her son, wispy and fine-boned, knew that she was so intent on listening for what she would never hear that his screams at night had all the relevance of a dream to her. The instant the night curfew was lifted the boy raced through the garden and out of the gate, his steps making crosses of Mrs Shaukut's footprints. The street no longer smelled of cricketer's sweat or garlands of motia, no longer bristled with the enmity of neighbouring cooks, but remained silent and still, pockmarked with bullet holes.

The boy ran past a shadow – all that remained of the car which had exploded at the edge of his vision three days earlier. A man, tapping his lighter against a hollow lamp-post, watched the boy run in his direction. The boy tripped, hit his chin on the handlebar of a bicycle. The man snapped open his lighter and, scant feet away, the boy's mouth filled with blood.

It had a metallic taste, the blood, and the boy didn't know if that was because of his braces, the bike's handlebar, or the man's lighter. He ran his tongue over his teeth and gums, searching for the wound, and found it, instead, on the underside of his lip. A year ago he would have made his way to the store at the street corner, and the shopkeeper would have told him to hold this ice-lolly, here, against the cut to staunch the flow of blood. He would have eaten the ice-lolly, his blood mixing pleasantly with the cold orange taste, and the shopkeeper would have teased him by calling out to the tailor across the street and saying the boy needed stitches.

But now there was only the boy, the man with the lighter, and the mother who was unable to recognize her neighbourhood's shift from community to battlefield as reality rather than yet another indicator of the madness her husband had diagnosed for her. She heard the crash of the bicycle as her son fell into the handlebar's embrace and pulled it down to the ground in a tangle of metal and limbs, but mistook it for the soundtrack in her mind replaying the accident on the way to the delivery room.

There was another crash: the bed in which they wheeled her through the hospital collided with a doorway swinging open to make way for the grief of a weeping girl.

The boy had watched the girl run out of the hospital building and wanted to follow her, calling out, 'I will marry you one day.' But instead he allowed the nurses to take him to a room with crayons and plastic blocks, where he drew a red bicycle and imagined riding down the street with the girl running alongside him.

All these last months as the neighbourhood emptied itself of familiarity he had been praying for the girl to appear, a green skipping rope trailing from her hand (he didn't know why he longed to see her with a skipping rope, let alone a green one, but this is how she appeared to him when he closed his eyes and he knew better than to question the strange precision of desire). But after all that praying and all that dreaming, he had conjured up only this man with flint eyes who continued to tap his lighter against the lamp-post, his eyes shifting from the boy incarnadining the white shirt sleeve he held against his mouth to the group of boys who turned down the side street and made their way to Mrs Shaukut's house, their postures exactly what you would expect of boys who had a common cause for an hour each day and were, at all other hours, watching each other's families drown one another in a blood feud. They each wore the white of mourners; not one of them had escaped a funeral that morning.

The eldest of the group felt as though he were walking apart from the others even though he was in the centre of the group, carefully cradling a dozen eggs in his hands. His beard was beginning to come in and yesterday he had, for the first time, taken apart a gun and put it back together, its weight in his hands greater than when his brothers and uncles assembled it; his brothers had laughed and slapped him on the back when he said as much. It was the added weight of his emotions, they said.

The eldest boy knew today was his last time as part of this group which he had first organized. Tomorrow he would be cradling a gun in his now egg-laden hands, and his responsibilities would shift elsewhere. Today was a stolen day of childhood; by rights he should already be on the back of a motorcycle, gun concealed under shawl, waiting for the moment his oldest living brother, bent low over the handlebar, shouted 'Now!' But his brothers had argued with their uncles to allow him this final day as egg-bearer. The brothers, too, had been taught by Mrs Shaukut and, besides, they knew how profoundly the youngest male of their clan loved the teacher who had never laughed at him for being an eight-year-old in a classroom full of five-year-olds. When he had finished assembling the gun yesterday, the satisfaction of hearing that click as the barrel slotted into place reminded him of the sensation of looking at a series of curlicues on a page and knowing for the first time, this is a word and it spells 'dog'. Because that knowledge had come to him later than to the other boys, he had not yet learnt to take it for granted, so as he walked down the street his eyes were alert for language, his lips and tongue shaped themselves around the messages on billboards and the names outside desolate houses.

If he had been looking less intently for words and more intently for objects, he would have noticed the man at the end of the street with a lighter in one hand, the other hand resting beneath a shawl which was draped around his shoulders just so, requiring only a flick of a wrist to unwind it from his body and reveal the long-barrelled object hidden beneath the folds and drapes. But the egg-carrier, surrounded by boys of every family in the neighbourhood, could not conceive of this street, at this dawn hour, as anything but safety so his eyes travelled over the man and the boy and swerved around to return to Mrs Shaukut's gate.

'Tomorrow, you bring the eggs,' he called ahead to the second oldest in the group, the one whose father had been killed by his (the egg-carrier's) eldest brother. The second oldest put his hand to his chin, as though it were possible for stubble to have sprouted since he scrutinized his face in the mirror less than an hour ago. Encountering only the smoothness of skin, he nodded and pushed open Mrs Shaukut's gate. He walked to the end of his driveway and turned smartly on his heels to face the garden, the rest of the boys falling into place beside and behind him. They each placed their goods on the ground and stood at attention.

'Good morning, Mrs Shaukut,' they called out in unison to the woman in the garden with the vacant gaze. They had long since passed from expecting a response and recently had ceased to hope for one either. So as soon as the greeting was out of their mouths they turned again and made their way into her kitchen to fill the fridge with milk and eggs and bread (because the son knew what to do with those for breakfast) and containers filled with food that their mothers and sisters had cooked the night before. They checked the little cupboard above the stove, and the boy with top marks in the last handwriting exam that Mrs Shaukut had corrected took out his note pad and wrote down 'Supplies Needed' at the top of the page, and 'TEA' beneath it. When he finished he stood with pencil at the ready, waiting to write down anything else that the other boys, some of them now making their way through the house, might call out. Washing powder, or toilet paper, or cold cream, perhaps. While he waited, the boy turned to look out of the window and saw the man with a lighter, his shawl thrown off, standing in the driveway, camera moving from Mrs Shaukut to the boys picking leaves out of the flower-bed to the kitchen window through which the boy with the beautiful handwriting was looking out.

The boy with the beautiful handwriting called out to Mrs Shaukut's son, who was standing next to the man with the lighter, watching him. Mrs Shaukut's son shrugged and the boy with the beautiful handwriting pressed his pencil to the paper, in his 'Get Set' mode, just in time to hear a boy from upstairs shout down, 'Butterscotch sweets. Again.' The boy with the beautiful handwriting glanced at Mrs Shaukut's son, who rocked back on his heels in a manner too adult for his age and tried not to look guilty. The taste of butterscotch was all that remained to him now of his former life, and several times a day he would hold a sweet in his mouth against the warmth of his cheek, touching his tongue to it for long intervals to taste childhood.

'Who have you lost?' the boy asked the man who had put away his lighter to hold a camera in both hands, and was moving forward to get as close to Mrs Shaukut as he judged the boys in the garden would allow.

The man raised his face above the camera and looked at the boy. 'My wife. Five weeks ago. How did you know?'

The boy bent down to uproot a blade of grass and, straightening, stroked his bloodied lip with its tip. 'My mother has turned this neighbourhood into a metaphor for grief. That's what my father said before he left.'

The man knew that the father had told the doctors in the emergency room, 'If it's a girl, save the mother so she can bear me more sons. The one I have now is sickly and given to dreaming.' He wondered if the boy knew it, too. In that moment of imagining the boy's life he said, 'Come away from here with me,' and surprised only himself.

The boy smiled. 'You can't just walk out of metaphors. If my mother had taught you, you'd know that.'

The man squatted down so he was looking up into the boy's eyes, a supplicant. 'How then?' And his hands were shaking.

'I'm just a boy,' the boy said.

The man lowered his knees to the ground and placed the camera down. His hands were empty and he brought them together, one palm resting on top of the other. For months now the brave and desperate among the photojournalists had been making their way here, searching for some understanding. Why had the schoolteacher's accident unleashed such violence in the neighbourhood, each family claiming to have seen in a neighbouring house the driver who ran away from the scene of the crime?

The man raised his eyes to Mrs Shaukut, who was still standing beside the hibiscus, brushing her hand against the ragged red petals. She heard him cry out, 'When will you stop this?' but it meant nothing to her, nor did the touch of the eldest boy as he bent down and rested his fingertips against her foot for the briefest moment.

The eldest boy stood up, took one last look at her and walked towards the gate. On his way out he stopped and said to the kneeling man with the hands of prayer, 'When enough of us have died for all parents to wish only for daughters, that's when she'll stop.'

'That could take a thousand years,' the man said, weeping now.

The eldest boy laughed softly. 'She doesn't lack patience.'

He walked away, his hands practising the motion of unravelling a shawl and raising a gun as a soldier might practise a salute or a boy his morning greeting to a beloved teacher.

Tahar Ben Jelloun

from The Rising of the Ashes

This body that was a body will no longer stroll the length
   of the Tigris or the Euphrates
loaded by a shovel that will not remember
   a single painput in a black plastic bag
this body that was a soul, a name and a face
turned over to face the ground of sands
detritus and absence.

*

I am sleeping in other bodies emptied
      of their entrails
they were still warm
the one that moves does not have an arm
it is a starving cat struck by lightning.

*

After 'Guernica' (1937) — Beirut, Cana, Tyr (2006)

They tell me: the grief for us is in
    the gaze of our children.
Who will tell them the history of our defeats?
Will they believe us?
I see them spit on the defunct faces
so many useless verbs.
Oh the verb, the words, the litany of the famished
bitter bread buried in the low land
I see them run to pick up our worn-out shoes
they make a fire with the poems written by
    the generals
and burn our memory.
They did not spit any longer.
They do not speak anymore.
They forget.

*

We have gotten astray.
We have been for a long time.
Our guides walk on our shoulders.
They are always armed.
They do not know how to sing or dance
but they write sentimentalizing poems
and uninspired discourses.
They spit on anonymous faces
as in the festivals of ancient times.

Translated by Cullen Goldblatt

Jung Chang

from Wild Swans

The day after I returned to school, I was taken out with several dozen other children to change street names to make them more 'revolutionary'. The street where I lived was called Commerce Street, and we debated what it should be renamed. Some proposed 'Beacon Road', to signify the role of our provincial Party leaders. Others said 'Public Servants' Street', as that was what officials should be, according to a quote of Mao's. Eventually we left without settling on anything because a preliminary problem could not be solved: the name plate was too high up on the wall to reach. As far as I knew, no one ever went back.

In Peking the Red Guards were much more zealous. We heard about their successes: the British mission was now on 'Anti-Imperialism Road', the Russian embassy on 'Anti-Revisionism Road'.

In Chengdu, streets were shedding their old names like 'Five Generations under One Roof' (a Confucian virtue), 'The Poplar and Willow Are Green' (green was not a revolutionary color), and 'Jade Dragon' (a symbol of feudal power). They became

'Destroy the Old', 'The East Is Red', and 'Revolution' streets. A famous restaurant called 'The Fragrance of Sweet Wind' had its plaque broken to bits. It was renamed 'The Whiff of Gunpowder'.

Traffic was in confusion for several days. For red to mean 'stop' was considered impossibly counterrevolutionary. It should of course mean 'go'. And traffic should not keep to the right, as was the practice, it should be on the left. For a few days we ordered the traffic policemen aside and controlled the traffic ourselves. I was stationed at a street corner telling cyclists to ride on the left. In Chengdu there were not many cars or traffic lights, but at the few big crossroads there was chaos. In the end, the old rules reasserted themselves, owing to Zhou Enlai, who managed to convince the Peking Red Guard leaders. But the youngsters found justifications for this: I was told by a Red Guard in my school that in Britain traffic kept to the left, so ours had to keep to the right to show our anti-imperialist spirit. She did not mention America.

As a child I had always shied away from collective activity. Now, at fourteen, I felt even more averse to it. I suppressed this dread because of the constant sense of guilt I had come to feel, through my education, when I was out of step with Mao. I kept telling myself that I must train my thoughts according to the new revolutionary theories and practices. If there was anything I did not understand, I must reform myself and adapt. However, I found myself trying very hard to avoid militant acts such as stopping passers-by and cutting their long hair, or narrow trouser legs, or skirts, or breaking their semi-high-heeled shoes.

Madi
Beirut café

Shirin Neshat
Anchorage

Displaced children in Lebanon, aged 4–9 years, in painting (top) and music (bottom) workshops organized by Masrah al-Madina in Beirut.

The following are paintings by displaced Lebanese children (from the workshops organized by Masrah al-Madina).

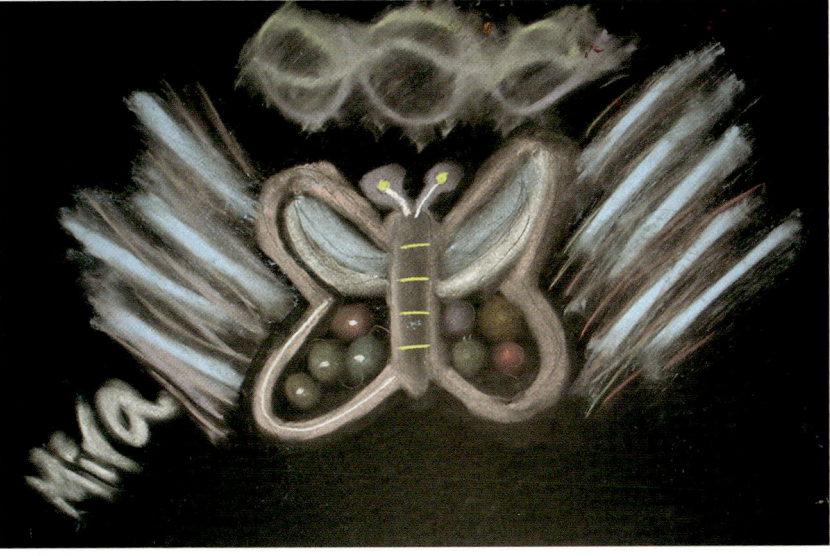

These things had now become signs of bourgeois decadence, according to the Peking Red Guards.

My own hair came to the critical attention of my schoolmates. I had to have it cut to the level of my earlobes. Secretly, though much ashamed of myself for being so 'petty bourgeois,' I shed tears over losing my long plaits. As a young child, my nurse had a way of doing my hair which made it stand up on top of my head like a willow branch. She called it 'fireworks shooting up to the sky'. Until the early 1960s I wore my hair in two coils, with rings of little silk flowers wound around them. In the mornings, while I hurried through my breakfast, my grandmother or our maid would be doing my hair with loving hands. Of all the colors for the silk flowers, my favorite was pink.

Adam Nankervis
Bridge

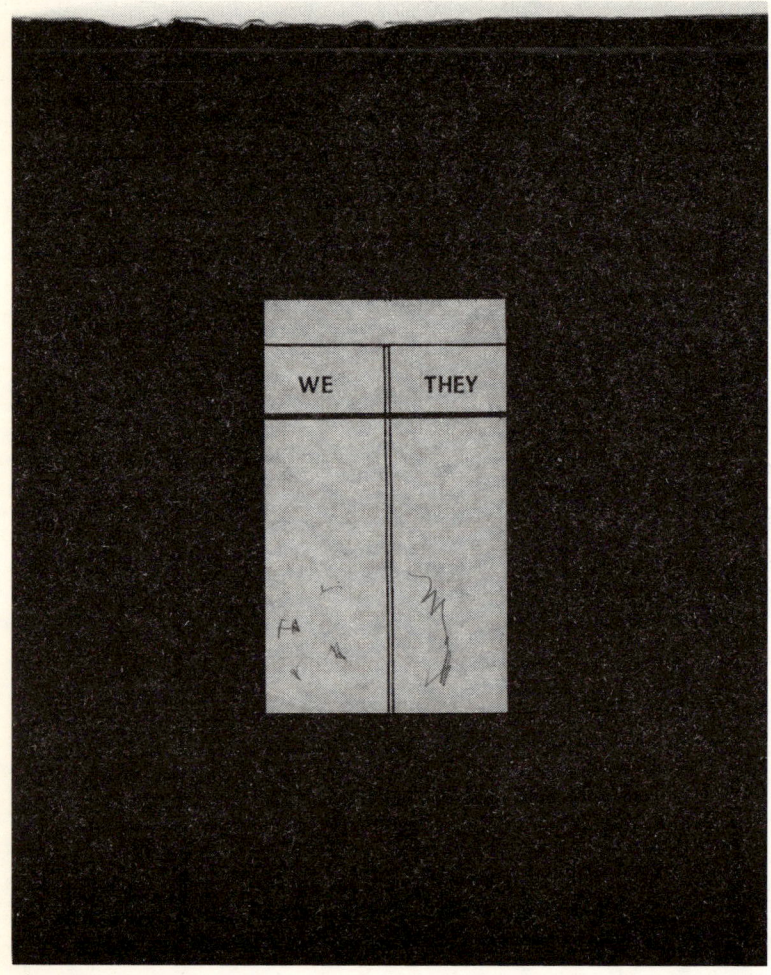

Beverley Naidoo

The Crocodile and the Stork

Stork was in mourning. Her black feathers hung like a cloak around her white breast. Crying had made her eyes as blood red as her long beak. But tears could not bring back her babies. She was resolved to have her revenge on Crocodile, who had raided her nest.

'Crocodile shall cry tears like mine,' she vowed.

Every day she waited for hours in the reeds beside the water. The leg on which she stood was as still as a reed itself. Only in the evening shadows, when hunger made her feel faint, did her beak strike down like an arrow to catch one or two fish. Afterwards, she returned to her mute pose.

From her hiding place she saw where Crocodile hid her eggs in a hole on the riverbank. Patiently Stork waited, day after day, until the young had hatched. Silently she watched Crocodile carry the first baby in her mouth and lower it gently into the water. Stork remained perfectly quiet. As soon as the little crocodile began to swim away from the bank, its mother set off for her nest to collect another. Stork saw her chance and swooped. Lifting the crocodile baby in the cradle of her beak, she flew down the river and dropped it into an empty animal pen at the edge of a village. By the time the baby shrieked, its mother was too far away to hear.

One by one, while Crocodile's back was turned, Stork captured every one of her twelve babies. When Crocodile realised that they had all disappeared, she screeched with rage and pain. Stork now flew up into a tree above the riverbank.

'Have you seen my children?' Crocodile cried. Giant tears welled up in her eyes.

'Oh yes,' Stork replied. 'I have taken them.'

'Where are they?' Crocodile roared. 'Give them back or I'll—'

'If you want them back, you will have to bring me seventy fish for each child,' Stork said calmly.

Crocodile gnashed her teeth and whipped her tail but, in the end, it was agreed that the exchange would take place three days later. Crocodile knew that she would have to work night and day to collect enough fish in time.

On the day of the exchange, Crocodile pulled her heavy basket of fish upstream towards the appointed place. On the way, she passed some villagers plucking a large bird near a fire. A small gust of wind caught one of the feathers and blew it towards Crocodile. It was a long, black feather. Fear lodged in Crocodile's throat. She swam closer to the shore and, sure enough, the bird that the villagers were preparing to roast was Stork! Crocodile wept tears of fury. She knew that she would never see her babies again. With a heavy heart, she turned away, swearing to kill all those who ate the bird that had stolen her babies.

Alberto Manguel

Once Again, Troy

When I think of Beirut, three images come to mind. The first is the one my mother described to me after visiting the city in the early fifties. She had been to Paris, to Rome, to Venice; she thought there was no city as lovely as Beirut, as elegant, as welcoming. Whenever things would go wrong in Buenos Aires (and they would go wrong often) she would complain and shake her head and, instead of repeating, 'Moscow, Moscow!' like one of Chekhov's three sisters, she would sigh, 'Beirut, Beirut!', as if her life in that paradise would have been different had she stayed. Perhaps it would have, because Beirut was for her an impossibility, and impossible things tend to be perfect.

The second image is that of the city I visited in 2004. The friendship of the people, their extraordinary courtesy, the constant shift in tone bred from the variety of cultural backgrounds, the pride and relief in seeing their city built up again after the war, the lack of shame with which they showed their scars, their ingrained and shared belief in the vital importance of poetry, music, good food, intelligent conversation, left me, as I returned home, with a sudden nostalgia for what I had experienced as civilisation.

The third image is the bombed city I see now, in the evening news. Like any ravaged city, it is both a place of incommunicable daily personal suffering and also the image of every city in no-matter-what war; a place in which walls that took so long to build lie crumbled in the streets and someone stares at a fallen roof underneath which lies a brother, a sister, a friend, a parent, a child, and soldiers race past.

There is a fourth Beirut, I think. It is made less of stones rebuilt and stones demolished, than of the perseverance of memory. In one of the last books of *The Iliad*, the murderous Achilles runs after Hector, the murderer of Achilles' friend Patroclus. Both are soldiers, both have blood on their hands, both have loved ones who have been killed, both believe that their cause is just. One is Greek, the other Trojan, but at this point their allegiances hardly matter. They are two men intent on killing one another. They run past the city walls, past the double springs of the river Scamander. And at this point, Homer (the ancient presence we call Homer) breaks off his description and pauses to remind us (the translation is by Robert Fagles):

> *And here, close to the springs, like washing-pools*
> *scooped out in the hollow rocks and broad and smooth*
> *where the wives of Troy and their lovely daughters*
> *would wash their glistening robes in the old days,*
> *the days of peace before the sons on Achaea came ...*
> *Past there they raced*

Past there they raced

Claudia Roden

Mezze in the Bekaa Valley

I recently visited Zahle, the world capital of the Arab *mezze* – it had long been one of my dreams. Many of my relatives in Egypt had been regular visitors to the mountain resort in the Bekaa Valley in Lebanon (it was our Switzerland) and they always came back with fantastic stories of the unending assortments of *mezze* they were offered in the cafés along the river Berdawni that cascades down the mountain. Zahle has since acquired a mythical reputation for gastronomy, and some of its local dishes have come to represent the standard menu of Lebanese restaurants around the world.

This is how it happened: the drinking of *arak*, the anis-flavoured spirit, is behind the philosophy and practice of the *mezze* tradition, and it is produced in Zahle, where the main Lebanese wines are also produced. The tradition, a national institution that represents a convivial art of living, developed as a way of soaking up the powerful drink, affectionately called 'lion's milk' because it turns cloudy when water and ice are added. In 1920 the first two cafés opened by the river. They gave away nuts, seeds, olives, and bits of cheese with the local *arak*.

Gradually, the entire valley became filled with open-air cafés, each larger and more luxurious than the next, each vying with ever more varied *mezze* to attract customers who flocked from all over the Middle East. The reputation of the mountain village foods spread far and wide, and they became the model for the burgeoning restaurant trade.

Picking at a variety of foods is a wonderful way to eat, but the spirit of fun and conviviality attached to the *mezze* is just as important, and there is plenty of that in Lebanon. I was taken to the Bekaa Valley by Kamal Mouzawak – the food writer and TV chef who is the local co-ordinator of the Slow Food movement – and his fashion designer partner, Rabih Kayrouz. We were there for a wedding party near the ancient city of Baalbek (it was garlanded with Hizbullah flags and portraits of the assassinated Palestinian Sheikh Yassin). Nadim Khattar, a London-based architect, and Andrea Kowalski, a Venezuelan working at the BBC, had organised a fantastic feast in a field in the middle of the countryside for their guests who came from all over the world (Fergus Henderson of St John's restaurant was there with his extended family). The lunch went on for hours as little dish upon little dish arrived at the long tables, one more exquisite than the other, each jostling for space, while baby lambs roasted on fires and musicians played. It was more wonderful than any image I had of Bekaa in my childhood. The wedding party went on for two days, moving on to the old Palmyra hotel. I returned with the Hendersons and with the painter Ffiona Lewis. We stopped for a *mezze* lunch in Zahle. It is now a town full of concrete housing overlooked by a giant statue of the Virgin Mary perched on the mountainside, but its riverside restaurants still offer a marvellous range of *mezze*.

Wedding celebrations continued in Beirut. An impromptu dinner for sixty remaining guests (I helped to cook) was at Kamal and Rabih's. They are famous for the dinner parties they hold in their old-style apartment and roof garden. I came back to London vowing to adopt the *mezze* habit – the spirit as well as the dishes.

Owen Sheers

Watching

The restaurant was a surprise. A low, peach-coloured bungalow isolated at the side of the road outside the village of Jamestown, County Leitrim. Everything else in that evening scene was to be expected. The silhouettes of the three men fishing on a curve in the river; the static of the white-watered weir; the black lung of a starling roost expanding and contracting on the breeze; the somnambulant slide of the Shannon, flowing north at the only point in its 250 mile course through this country. But the peach bungalow with a sign outside reading 'Al Mezza, Lebanese Restaurant', here in the middle of the fields and the sheep, that was a surprise.

As we sit at our table Dorothy Serhan hands us a menu each, opening them as she does as if presenting us with velvet boards of jewellery. On the first page there is a map of Lebanon. I catch my girlfriend's eye and register our shared reaction. A month ago, when we left London to travel through Europe, this map would have been unfamiliar to us. We would only have known the names of its capital and perhaps the rough outline of its borders. But now, after the last three weeks of watching

TV screens in hotels, bars and airport lounges, we are all too familiar with this map, and especially the names of its southern towns and villages. Tyre, Mansoura, Bent Jbail, Quaraoun. After three weeks of watching a war, we not only know the locations of these places, the beaches they overlook and the hills at their backs. We also know how many people have been killed in each of them. If we tried hard enough we could probably even remember where they'd been sheltering when they died, how many children had been in the family or what kind of a car had been taking them away when the driver had glimpsed, for a tenth of a second in the rear view mirror, the missile, before it obliterated them entirely.

I look up from the menu at the framed photographs of Beirut cityscapes hanging over each table. The views of this city are also familiar to us now, although the ones we've seen have looked less and less like these photographs every day. Here, in the picture frames on the walls of Al Mezza in Jamestown, Beirut is a living city; the circuit board of high-rise buildings at night, mast lights reflected in the water of a harbour, a main street coloured with people, stalls, cars and scooters. The Beirut we have seen framed on those TV screens these past three weeks, however, has been a very different city. An empty city. A city with clouds of dark smoke hanging over its buildings. Its streets have been silent and blocks of its flats have been reduced to rubble, leaving gaps in the skyline like missing teeth in a mouth. There has nearly always been a news channel logo spinning in the bottom right hand corner and, usually, a flak-jacketed man or woman standing in the foreground describing in measured tones which part of the city behind them has been destroyed today. Sometimes we have seen the Beirut of these photographs framed in another way too: the dimensions of the city flattened to an overhead image of grainy monochrome, a hairline cross etched at its centre which, after waiting for a second or so, plants a sudden dark flower at its intersection that blossoms then fades among the rooftops and streets.

I look back down at my menu and begin to read the page opposite the map. 'The food of Lebanon,' it tells me, 'is a celebration of life; it is fresh, flavourful and invigorating.'

When Dorothy returns to take our order my girlfriend asks if she has any friends caught up in the fighting. 'Yes,' she says, tight-lipped as she pours a bottle of deep-red wine from the Bekaa valley. 'My husband's family are still there. My brother-in-law managed to get out though. He flew in from Syria yesterday.'

It is Dorothy's brother-in-law who serves us our starters, *Fattoush*, *Jawaneh*, *Sujok* and *Kallajjibneh*. For three weeks now we have watched the news coming out of Lebanon. For three weeks we have watched commentators and experts speak about Lebanon. For three weeks we have been intimate with the details of who has been killed, where and how. We have seen the grief cries of mothers; we have seen a man holding his daughter's lifeless hand, thick with a glove of dust, emerging from the rubble; we have seen a Brooklyn taxi driver who came to Beirut for a holiday, searching for his uncle and aunt in the remains of their flat. And now, serving at our table is a man who has come from that place, a man who, for us watchers, seems to have been born from the news. I can't help watching again as he moves through the restaurant, rows of white plates balanced along the inside of his forearms. The one piece of information Dorothy told us about him has electrified his quiet presence. But what do I expect to see? Some sign of the conflict on his face? A trace of the stresses and tremors of war in his expression? At times I think I catch a hint, the faintest quiver of it under his skin, but I know I'm imagining this. There is no sign of war upon him other than our knowledge of where he has come from.

The meal finishes with coffee; sweet, strong and flavoured with cardamom. 'Coffee is a big deal in Lebanon,' the menu tells me again. 'It is served throughout the day. When guests arrive at one's home, they are invariably persuaded to stay for a coffee, no matter how short their visit.'

When we leave Al Mezza later that night Dorothy calls for her husband Malid to come and say goodbye. He emerges from the kitchen in his chef's hat and tunic, bringing a scent of its heat and spices with him. We thank him for his food. Then we say we hope his family will be alright, that they will be safe. 'Yes,' he says with a tense smile, pushing his glasses up the bridge of his nose. 'So do I. But their home is gone. The family home is gone. It has been bombed, so they are in the hills now. They have some food from the fields and we are trying to arrange visas for them, but the children,' he pauses, looks down and wipes his hands on his tunic. 'Well the children are very frightened of course. When we speak to them on the phone we can hear the planes in the background, even there in the hills. The planes frighten them very much.' When Malid raises his head again there is a different look in his eyes as if he is watching something further away, beyond the restaurant, past the slow Shannon and the three men still fishing on her curve. All of us are silent for a moment. There is just the background chatter and clinking of people dining inside the restaurant, the hushing of the weir outside. Dorothy also looks away for a moment. I can feel the heat of her quiet anger emanating off her, like the heat of the kitchen emanating off Malid's tunic. 'It is so frustrating,' he says eventually with both a sigh and a smile at the same time. 'Innocents are dying on both sides. Innocents,' he says again, looking back at us and shaking his head slightly. 'On both sides. While the world watches.'

It isn't until we are in a cab being driven along the winding country road back into Jamestown that I realise, just like with the map in the menu and the framed views of Beirut, I am already familiar with what Malid has just said to us. I have heard it before, but in a different language, in different words, just last week when I saw Condoleezza Rice on one of those hotel TV screens, when I watched her step up to the microphone at a press conference and explain why now was not the right time to call for an immediate ceasefire. Of course, although I heard Condoleezza's words I didn't really *see* them back then, and I doubt she did either. And because I didn't see them, I didn't really understand what they meant, until I heard Malid describe them again tonight. But that is because Condoleezza's language has long ago become dislocated from meaning, while Malid's has not.

The cab drives on, winding its way between the ancient oaks

at the side of the road. As we pass an inland lake the driver taps his knuckle against the inside of his window. 'Look at that moon,' he says. 'When did you last see a moon like that?' I look out at the moon, full, pitted and startlingly white above the ink-black lake in which it sheds its reflection like a skin. My girlfriend does not look at the moon. Her head is bent over and she is crying, for Malid's nieces and nephews, frightened by the warplanes in the hills above Beirut. The cab drives on, the white dashes in the road slipping under its headlights as my girlfriend and I make promises; to send money, to contribute to a charity, to write to an MP, to do anything, something. For now though, as the houses of Jamestown grow about us, I just hold her in the back of the cab, watching the moon rise higher in the sky, ridiculously grateful that I can at least do that.

it is not us who
    invaded PALESTINE
it is not us who did
        the HOLOCAUST
it is not us who killed
        the ARMENIANS
it is not us who did
        the 11th SEPTEMBER
it is not us who did
        the ISLAMIC REVOLUTION
it is not us who
    invented NUCLEAR BOMBS
it is not us who
    poisoned SNOW WHITE
Can't you leave us
        ALONE for a while?

Brian Whitaker

I Half-expected John Wayne

There were about thirty of us waiting for the seven am flight from Amman to Beirut. The plane was waiting too and a man in a wheelchair had been moved to the door of the departure lounge, ready for boarding. Seven o'clock came but nothing happened. Five past. Ten minutes past. Seven-fifteen.

One of the passengers phoned a friend in Lebanon. He hung up and said, 'The Israelis are bombing Beirut airport.' Eventually an official appeared, took away our boarding cards, gave us our tickets back and told us, more or less, to get lost. He had no idea when flights to Beirut might resume and, as events turned out, there were none for the next thirty-five days. I had set off for Lebanon just a few hours after Hizbullah seized two Israeli soldiers on the border. It was not the first incident of its kind but, coming so soon after Hamas's abduction of another soldier, and with Israel threatening to teach Lebanon a 'sharp lesson', the repercussions were obviously going to be more serious than usual. Just how serious was yet to be seen. We hung around the airport for a while, debating what to do. There were several other journalists among us and eventually we decided to head for Lebanon by road. The only problem was that we would have to pass through Syria. None of us had visas, and getting them can be tricky for journalists. A phone call to the Syrian embassy in Amman was not encouraging: 'We can't issue visas to journalists in Jordan,' an official said. 'You must go back to London and apply there.'

At a taxi office near Abdali bus station plastered with signs saying 'al-Sham, Beirut', the man in charge was more hopeful. 'British passport OK. American, no,' he said. An American from the *New York Times* was undeterred. His paper knew a Syrian fixer in London, he said. All you had to do was pay him two hundred US dollars and a visa was guaranteed. With no better alternative than to kick our heels in Amman, we headed for the border to see what would happen. After officially leaving Jordan it was a short drive through no-man's land to the Syrian passport office which was crammed with people pushing and shoving to get to the windows. We went to the one labelled 'Diplomats and Investors' where the crowd was indistinguishable from the rest but the crush was slightly less. The man behind the window looked at my application form, then handed it back. 'We can't give visas to journalists,' he said, repeating what the embassy had told us. 'But I don't want to stay in Syria,' I explained. 'I was on my way to Beirut and the Israelis started bombing the airport.' He looked thoughtful for a moment, then went off to make a phone call. 'If we give you a visa,' he said on returning, 'will you promise to report to the Ministry of Information in Damascus before you leave the country?' I readily agreed and he stamped my passport with a satisfying thud. No need for *wasta* and no need for a two hundred dollar payment to the mysterious man in London; just explanation of the unusual circumstances.

Government bureaucracy bedevils Syria, like many Arab countries, but when war came to Lebanon it proved remarkably flexible. They cut the red tape, not only bending the rules to let journalists and aid workers pass through but also to welcome the vast numbers of Lebanese citizens who fled the bombing. Returning to Syria from Lebanon just over a fortnight later, I stopped at a street stall for a falafel sandwich. Chatting with the man as he prepared it, I mentioned that I had just arrived from Beirut – and he promptly declined payment. 'It's a gift,' he said, offering me a free drink to go with it. Of course there was an element of politics in all this, but also genuine human sympathy. Thousands of ordinary Syrians opened up their homes to take in Lebanese refugees.

Entering Lebanon after the first night's bombing, we descended into the Bekaa, with the fields spread out before us on the valley floor looking remarkably tranquil. It was a beautiful afternoon and we relaxed at a café over juice and *manouche* (thyme or cheese pastry) before resuming our journey over the mountains. The only indication that anything was amiss as we approached Beirut came from the cars travelling in the opposite direction, many of them crammed with families: not the mass exodus that occurred over the following days, but already a steady flow. I checked in to the Commodore Hotel which, as the Beirutis fled, rapidly filled up with foreigners carrying TV cameras. It had been a regular media haunt during the civil war, as my *Guardian* colleague Martin Woollacott once described:

> After the fighting in the Lebanese civil war led to the destruction of more famous and luxurious hotels on the Beirut Corniche, the Commodore became the hotel of choice for journalists. Its location deep in West Beirut, tucked between taller buildings that usually took the brunt of any shell or mortar fire, was safer in the physical sense. Thanks to the astuteness of the Palestinian Christian family that owned the hotel and that of the manager, Fuad, it was usually safe, too, from the attentions of rival militia groups. All were assuaged, paid off, and occasionally wined and dined in a successful attempt to insure that, whatever else suffered in that quarter of Beirut, it was not the Commodore or its guests. Just in case, the reception staff kept Kalashnikov rifles and a few grenades behind the desk.

It was shortly after three am that the bombs awoke me. I started counting the blasts but soon lost track. From the window I could see ribbons of anti-aircraft fire dancing up into the sky, glowing red then fading into blackness. Most of the bombing was out of sight, behind the hotel, but then, off to the west, there was a boom and a whoosh, followed by clouds of smoke lit up by fire. The Israelis had hit one of the airport's fuel tanks. When daylight came, I went to view the damage. The fuel tank was still ablaze and the main airport road had been hit too. A whole section of bridge had been blown away, killing three Syrians who ran a coffee stall underneath.

In the southern suburbs a bomb had landed exactly in the centre of a crossroads and another had punched a circular hole in an elevated roadway, damaging homes and shops on either side. Residents were already hard at work clearing up the mess, sweeping up broken glass and trying to remove bits of debris hanging from the telephone wires. Beirut, over the years, has had more than its share of bombs, and the first instinct of most people is to get back to normal as quickly as possible. It was not immediately apparent how sustained and relentless the bombing was going to be this time. As the gravity of the situation dawned, people fled their homes by the thousand. By the fourth night of the war, five hundred from the Shia suburbs were sleeping out in Sanayeh Park, not far from the city centre. Arriving to take a look, I was greeted at the gate by someone I had interviewed a year earlier in totally different circumstances: Ghassan Makarem from Helem, the Lebanese gay and lesbian rights organisation. In the absence of any initiative from the government, Helem had got together with other groups to help the homeless families. Helem's office, just around the corner from the park, and still displaying posters about safer sex on its walls, had suddenly become the nerve centre for local relief operations. Inevitably, it is the dramatic events in a war – the death and destruction – that attract most attention, but that is only part of the story. Well away from the immediate threat of bombs, shops and other businesses closed as their customers disappeared or staff were unable to get to work. In Beirut one afternoon, I took a walk downtown to what is supposedly the business and financial hub of Lebanon, and found it closed. The streets radiating from the normally throbbing Place de l'Etoile were eerily silent and utterly deserted apart from a soldier here and there, and the occasional private security guard lounging in the shade. With the whole place to myself, I began to wonder if there was something everyone else knew that I didn't. It resembled that scene in cowboy films where everyone has rushed inside and bolted their doors before the gunfight. I half-expected John Wayne to swagger into view at one end of the street and Clint Eastwood at the other, twiddling revolvers around their index fingers. Others battled through as best they could. Café Younes, in one of Hamra's side streets, is a tiny place but with every kind of coffee imaginable: Colombian, Ethiopian, Guatemalan, Brazilian, iced, latte, espresso, cappuccino, or topped with caramel – and all roasted on the premises. It had stayed open throughout the civil war and now the original owner's son, Amin, was determined to do the same even though he had no idea when his next supplies of coffee might arrive. In the meantime, he published a fascinating blog – 'A Lebanese Café During the War' – recounting the conversations among his diverse group of customers. Around the corner, directly opposite the Commodore Hotel, Ammar, the owner of a souvenir shop, was developing a new line: T-shirts saying 'Press – do not shoot'. Hard as anyone might try to maintain a semblance of normal life, it became almost impossible as the bombardment that many had expected to be over in just a few days continued for a week, then another, then more than a month. Oddly, the bombs themselves were the easiest part to get used to; so long as you were far enough away, you just carried on reading the newspaper or with whatever you happened to be doing at the time. It was the relentlessness of it all – and wondering when it would end – that made people depressed, irritable and, above all, weary. One afternoon I visited Dina, who works for a publishing company. She was coming to the office every day, she said, not because she had much work to do but to get away from the family. Like many Lebanese, her home was now crammed with relatives from the south; there were not enough mattresses to go round, it was hard to get any sleep, and with so many people cooped up in the same small space it did not take much to start the kids screaming and the aunts and cousins bickering. 'I'm so tired,' said Dina. 'This is worse than the civil war. Much worse.' That, perhaps, was the Israelis' biggest miscalculation. If they had hoped the bombing would turn the rest of Lebanon against Hizbullah, they were mistaken. It was not only the killing of a thousand civilians that stuck in people's minds but a seemingly pointless choice of targets – like the visit from an Israeli helicopter specially to take pot-shots at the Beirut lighthouse. Whatever the private feelings about Hizbullah's behaviour, Israel's response created an overwhelming sense of solidarity – a feeling that the Lebanese people, regardless of sect or political persuasion, were in it together.

Iain Sinclair

Body Tourism

> *It's unimaginable. It'll come*
> (Anita Brookner)

News of this season's war comes over the horizon
without a ripple, blank as paperpulp
scorched hair, pork & petrol, hot black
spiral columns of harm:
2 cars broadside on desert highway, we salute
video tremor (undead with platinum credit),
it takes quality sound to ruin such a morning,
shingle scraped, Dutch wreckage
The poet in his current (too current) self-disguise
justifies the hole in the page
holds his spectacles in a very peculiar way
meat-gloves, old old
as he is, eyeless, freaked for random
acquaintance, blinking
journeyman up from Smoke,
odd combo, diamond sweatshirt and rather

slick (sharky) jacket, sentimental bite:
surrealist tearaway now elder statesman (extant)

Let in, sea doesn't care, the poet
he hears gulls sneeze through glass

Malu Halasa

Too Black, Too Strong

Public Enemy reminded me I was Arab. During my near decade as the doyenne of hip hop, rap and scratch, I interviewed posses of rappers, DJs, musicians and producers. The limit was twelve guys standing in a semi-circular room, spliffing up. I moved the mic from mouth to mouth. I reported from dodgy hotel rooms, London housing estates and gigs that began as block parties and grew into stadium affairs. There were good times and weird. Early one morning after Afrika Bambaataa played the Roxy, two homeboys threatened me with a broken bottle and received $6 for their troubles. One of them yelled afterwards, 'Don't cry, little girl'; the subtext being: it's business, nothing personal – like Lebanon.

By the late 1980s for a biography on Elijah Muhammad, leader of the black separatist religious movement, the Nation of Islam, I frequented the tables of Nation esoterica (pamphlets on mystical mathematics and Dr Yacoub's race experiments, incense and perfumes) manned by dreads in the NYC subways, on the advice of Public's political honcho Professor Griff. The Nation successfully wooed Muhammad Ali in the 1960s when Malcolm X was its most charismatic convert. After his assassination and the rise of Louis Farrakhan, The Nation fell into disrepute. It enjoyed a resurgence among hip-hoppers in the mid-1980s, but it was never going to make sense to someone like Puff Daddy.

Puff Daddy made little sense to me. Once rap bootied and blinged my attention strayed, but before I left for good I learned a vital lesson. I spent so much time in someone else's black history, it was time to investigate my own. My mother, a Filipina, didn't identify her blackness in white America until her African American colleagues fast tracked her – like helps like. With her Jackie Onassis suits, Mom could pass, while the exoticism of our family, decadent Filipinos on one side, poor, hungry farmers in the arid mountains of Jordan on the other, drove me and my sister Marni a little nuts. In the mid-west of the US where we grew up, our compact family had been overwhelmed by my father's emigrating Arab tribe who either lived with us or dominated Dad's free time with their precious sons, because all he had was stupid girls – foreign ones at that. For our father and his family, we weren't Arab enough. For our mother we were too Arab, so she fiercely protected us from the cardinal sin of our ethnicity: marrying a cousin.

Ironically she, not my father, laid the groundwork for our Arabicity: taking us to the Levant, in 1970, after Black September in Jordan, when Ramadan filled Damascus's ancient streets with fedayeen guerrillas and no women. I wore a pink minidress in Beirut and in Jordan we crossed the Allenby Bridge into Israel and Tel Aviv and back again on our way to catch a

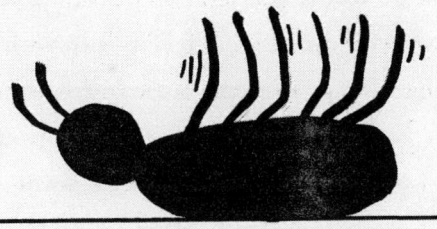

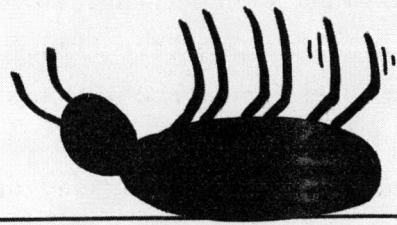

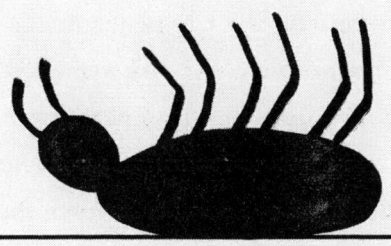

flight to Cairo. Each time dishy Israeli soldiers were suspicious of everything, even a box of Kotex pads. By 1979 I returned to the region by myself and did girl things: fell in love with a DFLP politico and searched for Arafat in war-scarred Beirut for a story that wouldn't be published until rap and rappers convinced me to mine my own experience. My Arabness was an internal journey but one I often compared. After a reading of diary extracts by Bethlehem teenagers, about living under the occupation, I sat in a circle of young Lebanese women, listening to their stories about the civil war: the interminable hours at home, the shelters and the fear. I knew then that my life as an Arab American had been safeguarded by virtue of an accident of birth and geography.

Now rap provides the soundtrack for the news. As I write, US-made Israeli drones fly over Beirut and the four thousand precision bombing operations taken place so far miss some of their targets in southern Lebanon. On the CD player are two Islamic girl rappers, Poetic Pilgrimage – '... My eyes don't see more than my heart can take/Listen/If you think a simple revolution can change the state, you're too late ...' When things require a loud screech of frustration, Fun-da-mental provides. I had taken the band's controversial CD All is War (The Benefits of G-had) to the US and first listened to the song 'I Reject' driving down Market St in Akron, Ohio, on 07.07.06, passing a line of strip malls and fast food restaurants made more surreal by switching on the radio and hearing BBC, not American, coverage of the bombings in London a year on. Since then not much has improved for Muslims – those who are inflamed are becoming more inflamed – or for London, now under continual terrorist threat.

'Arabs R the new Niggaz,' I told Fun-da-mental's Aki Nawaz, who argued against using so hateful a word. But I knew I wasn't wrong after reading the leftist Israeli writer Gideon Levy in *Ha'aretz*, 31.07.06, who writes, 'Since we've grown accustomed to thinking collective punishment a legitimate weapon, it is no wonder no debate has sparked here over the cruel punishment of Lebanon for Hizbullah's actions. If it was okay in Nablus, why not Beirut?' He then cites the reaction of fellow journalists and broadcasters to their country's offensive in Lebanon: 'Haim Ramon "doesn't understand" why there is still electricity in Baalbek; Eli Yishai proposes turning south Lebanon into a "sandbox"; Yoav Limor, a Channel 1 military correspondent, proposes an exhibition of Hizbullah corpses and the next day to conduct a parade of prisoners in their underwear "to strengthen the home front's morale".' If words fail, maybe an image will do: of burly, heavily armoured, helmeted US boys, guns akimbo, searching primitive stone structures in Ramadi, devoid of electricity and running water, with women and children in the dark and the dirt. Whether in the hands of the Israelis, Americans, Islamic regimes or all by themselves, Arab life has been cheapened and degraded. It is throwaway, unimportant.

When I returned to Beirut after the civil war I was overwhelmed by strangers who told stories about fast food, *tarab* and nose jobs. During that trip Nuha al-Radi, the author of *Baghdad Diaries* (who has since died of a disease not dissociated with depleted uranium, leukaemia), her sister Selma and their mother attended a lecture I gave at AUB, 'Memoir in the Time of Conflict'. Afterwards Selma told us about a US Predator drone in Yemen. Borrowing from Sven Lindquist's analysis of modern warfare, it was the latest technology in killing anonymously, murder from afar. Little did we know in 2002 that she was prophesying Lebanon's fate.

My husband and I were in Beirut in May. He and Nadine Touma from Dar Onboz scoured the streets for implements of a forgotten civil war for a joint project they were planning with stories, music and found objects. There wasn't a piece of scrap metal anywhere. The streets had been swept clean. That night Nadine drove us around the edges of her city. After the Israelis started attacking she wrote an open letter to friends, and it is only right to reproduce it here:

Dear Andy,

Do you remember when we were walking around in Beirut

Looking for junk yards, pieces of metal, shops of used things, things to create

your instruments that will illustrate and talk about my shelter story book on

my war in Beirut?

We couldn't find any.

This was two months ago.

You kept saying where is the junk in this city Nadine?

Well my dearest of all Andyz the good news is that now you have as much

Junk as you want and it is war junk the real stuff the hardcore authentic junk.

The sad news is that now there is no city!

PS. I promise to collect a few of my city junk for our book.

Bits of junk and old pop culture bind us together when governments, politicians and human rights fail.

Maggie Gee

Against Ending

Waking again from the book you look out of the window at stillness. The sunlight on the pavement lying pale and still as peace.

Stones which lie pale as peace – Unless you look you won't see them. Green fronds push through the cracks. Some children crouch on pale haunches.

Look at your hand, so peaceful. It lies on the page or the table. That hand has felt the warm sand run slow or fast through its fingers. The flesh looks so safe on the bone. And the children play on the pavement, counting on life going on.

To catch the sky in our hands. Endings that must not happen.

Birds, light-bodied and strong on the wind, make signs of love over London. Brave on the vast blind wind, over Lebanon, over London.

Words beat on against death.

Our bright lives beat against ending.

Always beginning again, beginning against ending.

Hugo Williams

Nothing in Particular

What do I miss?
I'll tell you what I miss –
the sun coming up,
colour starting,
a sort of yellow dust
or luminous moss
gathering round the edges
of table and chair,
a bedroom window sill
warming to the touch.

Everything soft as
soft rain
some average morning
when an upstairs window
catches the sun
and a young woman
turns back into a room,
or a telephone rings
and once again
she clears her throat.

Nothing in particular,
words, desires,
the slightest intention
translated into action,
the chain of command
taking shape in the mind
according to
logic and reason,
a tree coming into leaf,
our reward in heaven.

Hadrian Piggott
Cornish coast

Cornwall South Coast. 4 am Wednesday 9th August 2006

Two screaming jetfighters smear past, hurting the sky, and are gone ...

Imagine Lebanon .

Orhan Pamuk

To Read or not to Read
The Thousand and One Nights

I read my first tales from *The Thousand and One Nights* forty-odd years ago, when I was seven. I had just finished my first year of primary school and my brother and I had come to spend the summer in Geneva, Switzerland, where my parents had moved after my father took a job there. Amongst the books my aunt had given us on leaving Istanbul, to help us improve our reading over the summer, was a selection of stories from *The Thousand and One Nights*. It was a beautifully bound volume, printed on high quality paper, and I remember reading it four or five times over the course of the summer. When it was very hot, I would go to my room for a rest after lunch; stretching out in my bed, I would read the same stories over and over. Our apartment was one street away from the shores of Lake Geneva, and as a light breeze wafted in through the open window, and the strains of the beggar's accordion drifted up from the empty lot behind our house, I would drift off to lose myself in the land of Aladdin's Lamp and Ali Baba's Forty Thieves.

What was the name of the country I visited? My first

explorations told me it was alien and faraway, more primitive than our world, but part of an enchanted realm. You could walk down any street in Istanbul and meet people with the same names as the heroes, and perhaps that made me feel a little closer to them, but I saw nothing of my world in their stories – perhaps life was like this in the most remote villages of Anatolia, but not in modern Istanbul. So the first time I read *The Thousand and One Nights*, I read it like a Western child, amazed by the marvels of the East. I was not to know that its stories had long ago filtered into our culture from India, Arabia, and Iran, or that Istanbul, the city of my birth, was in many ways a living testament to the traditions from which these magnificent stories rose, or that their conventions – the lies, tricks, and deceptions, the lovers and betrayers, the disguises, twists and surprises – were deeply engrained in my native city's tangled and mysterious soul. It was only later that I discovered – from other books – that the first stories I read from *The Thousand and One Nights* had not been culled from the ancient manuscripts that Antoine Galland, the French translator, and the tales' first anthologiser, claimed to have acquired in Syria. Galland did not take Ali Baba and the forty thieves or Aladdin's magic lamp from a book – he heard them from a Christian Arab named Hanna Diyab and only wrote them down much later, when he was putting together his anthology.

This brings us to the real subject: *The Thousand and One Nights* is a marvel of Eastern literature. But because we live in a culture that has severed its links with its own cultural heritage and forgotten what it owes to India and Iran, surrendering instead to the jolts of western literature, it came back to us via Europe. Though it was published in many Western languages – sometimes translated by the finest minds of the age, and sometimes by the strangest, most deranged, and most pedantic – it is Antoine Galland's that was the most celebrated. At the same time, the anthology that Galland began to publish in 1704 is the most influential, most read, and most enduring. One could go so far as to say that it was the first time this endless chain of tales had appeared as a finite entity, and that it was in itself responsible for these stories achieving worldwide fame. The anthology exerted a rich and powerful influence on European writing for the better part of a century. The winds of a thousand and one nights rustle through the work of Stendhal, Coleridge, De Quincey and Edgar Allan Poe. But if we read the anthology from cover to cover, we can also see how that influence is bounded. It is preoccupied mostly with what we might call the 'mystical East' – for the stories are replete with miracles, strange and supernatural occurrences, and scenes of terror – but there is more to *The Thousand and One Nights* than that.

I could see this more clearly when I returned to *The Thousand and One Nights* in my twenties. This translation was by Raif Karada, who reintroduced the book to the Turkish public in the 1950s. Of course – like all intelligent readers – I didn't read it from cover to cover, preferring to wander from story to story as my curiosity took me. On second reading, the book troubled and provoked me. Even as I raced from page to page, gripped by suspense, I resented and sometimes truly hated what I was reading. That said, I never felt I was reading out of any sense of duty – as we sometimes do when reading classics – I read with great interest, but hating the fact that I was interested.

Thirty years later, I think I know what it is that was bothering me so much: in most of the stories, men and women were perpetually at war. I was unnerved by their neverending round of games, tricks, deceptions, and provocations. In the world of *The Thousand and One Nights*, no woman can ever be trusted – you can't believe a thing they say – they do nothing but trick men with their little games and ruses. It begins on the first page, as Sheherazade keeps a loveless man from killing her by entrancing him with stories. If this pattern is repeated through the book, it can only reflect how deeply and fundamentally men feared women in the culture that produced it. This is only reinforced by the fact that the weapon women use most successfully is their sexual charm. In this sense, *The Thousand and One Nights* is a powerful expression of the most potent fear entertained by men of that era: that women might abandon them, cuckold them, and condemn them to solitude. The story that provokes this fear most intensely – and affords the most masochistic pleasure – is the story of the sultan who watches his entire harem cuckold him with their black slaves. It confirms all the worst male fears and prejudices about the female sex, and so it is no accident that the popular 'social realist' novelist Kemal Tahir chose to milk this tale for all it was worth. But when I was in my twenties, and riddled with very male fears about never-to-be-trusted women, I found such tales suffocating, excessively 'oriental' and even somewhat coarse. In those days, *The Thousand and One Nights* seemed to pander too much to the tastes and preferences of the backstreets. The coarse, the two-faced, the evil – if they weren't ugly all along, they dramatised their moral depravity by becoming ugly – they were unremittingly repugnant, acting out their worst attributes over and over, just to keep the story alive.

It could be that the distaste I felt upon reading *The Thousand and One Nights* for the second time rose from the 'puritan streak' that sometimes afflicts westernising countries. In those days, young Turks like me who considered themselves 'modern' viewed the classics of Eastern literature as one might a dark and impenetrable forest. What we lacked, you might say, was a key – a way into this literature that preserved our modern outlook but still allowed us to appreciate its virtues.[1]

It was only when I read *The Thousand and One Nights* for the third time that I was able to warm to it. But this time I wanted to understand what it was that had so fascinated Western writers of its age – what had made the book into a classic. I saw it now as a great sea of stories – a sea with no end – what fascinated me were its assertions and its secret internal geometry. As before, I jumped from story to story at whim, abandoning one story midway if it started to bore me and moving to another. Though I had decided that it wasn't the stories' content that interested me so much as their shape, their proportions, their passions, it was, in the end, the stories' backstreet flavour that most appealed to me – those same evil details that I had once so deplored. Perhaps this had something

---

1. Literal translation: we did not have in our hands the modern keys that would allow us to approach and love it.

to do with the fact that I had lived long enough to know that life is made of treachery and malice. So on my third reading, I was finally able to appreciate *The Thousand and One Nights* as a work of art, to enjoy its timeless games of logic, of disguises, of hide-and-seek, and its many stories in which people pretend to be someone other than themselves. In my novel, *The Black Book*, I drew upon the magnificent story of Harun Reshit, who goes out in disguise one night to watch his double, the false Harun Reshit, impersonate him; I changed the story only to give it the feel of one of those black and white films of 1940s Istanbul. With the help of guidebooks written in English, I was able, by the time I was in my mid-thirties, to read *The Thousand and One Nights* for its secret logic, its inside jokes, its richness, its strangeness, its beauties tame and strange, its uglinesses, its impudences, its vulgarity – it was, in short, a treasure chest. My earlier love-hate relationship with the book no longer mattered: the child who could not recognise his world in it was a child who had not yet accepted life as it was, and the same could be said of the angry adolescent who dismissed it as vulgar. For I have slowly come to see that unless we accept *The Thousand and One Nights* as it is, it will – like life, when we refuse to accept it as it is – continue to be a source of great unhappiness. The reader should approach the book without hope or prejudice, and read it as he pleases, following his own whims, his own logic. Though perhaps I am already going too far – for it would be wrong to send a reader into this book with any preconceived ideas at all.

I would still like to use this book to say something about

reading and death. There are two things people always say about *The Thousand and One Nights*. One is that no one has ever managed to read the book from start to finish. The second is that anyone who does read *The Thousand and One Nights* from start to finish is sure to die. Certainly an alert reader who has seen how these two warnings fit together will wish to proceed with caution. But there's no reason for fear. Because we're all going to die one day, whether we read *The Thousand and One Nights* or not.

A thousand and one nights ...

Translated by Maureen Freely

Doris Lessing

'I Won't Ever Cry Again'

They were all working as fast as they could, but now water was rushing in to the centre of the shattered not-glass. Dann grabbed at the last of the books that were still dry, and leaped back as a jet of water shot up.

'That's it,' shouted Griot. 'General, we must run for it.'

Dann set down his final armful of books. The scribes were trying to sort the books into languages they knew, but the frail old things were falling apart. As each was opened, it began to crumble. Dann, desperate, grief-stricken, grabbed up book after book and saw it disintegrate in his hands. Fragments of paper bronzed and darkened as the air took it.

'And there goes the wisdom of a hundred civilisations,' said Dann. 'Look, there it goes. Going, going, gone.'

Dann was moving from table to table, hoping perhaps that at this one or that the books were still whole. He gently opened one after another, and watched it die, while odd words or lines of words sprang up clear and strong, like lines of writing being consumed by fire. Then he reached for another.

He was weeping. All the scholars working there in the hall

were desperate, some crying, some trying to catch the fragments of paper as they blew about.

Dann stood watching, Tamar behind him, and then from the direction of the secret room there came a noise like a clang, that gurgled into silence. The not-glass cell had spoken its last. From its direction crept a trickle of water.

'It's time we all left,' said Griot.

All along the hall the scribes were scribbling down odd phrases, even words, as the books fell into dust in their hands.

... truths to be self evident ...

Un vieux faun de terre cuite ...

... be in England ...

... Rose, thou art sick ...

... all the oceans ...

... rise from the dead to say the sun is shining ...

... into a summer's day ...

... Helen ...

Western wind, when ...

The Pleiades ...

... and I lie here alone ...

... and all roads lead to ...

'Dann, sir, what has been made can be made again,' said Griot.

'And again, and again, and again,' said Dann.

He sat at his table and Ali's, and watched the people all down the hall scurrying and scrabbling over the bits of browning paper.

'It's the again and again, Griot. I can never understand why you don't see it.'

Griot sat down near Dann. 'Sir, you make things so hard for yourself.'

Tamar sat down too. In her hand was a bit of crumbling paper. She was crying. She said, 'When I get to Tundra I won't ever cry again. Never.'

Moris Farhi

Tomorrow

Yesterday the poet al-Ma'arri told us
there were two kinds of leaders
those with brains and no religion
and those with religion and no brains
yet many people somehow survived
there were still
the skies
the sun
the sea
mountains and forests
love for life and wisdom to create
and myths and prophecies
that promised clement times

Today unquiet souls warn us
leaders have congealed into one kind
those with no religion and no brains
yet the people strive to survive
and

the skies
the sun
the sea
mountains and forests
love for life and wisdom to create
are still here
defiant
and myths and prophecies
of clement times
are still remembered

Tomorrow the unborn will say
there are
no skies
no sun
no sea
no mountains and forests
no love for life and no wisdom to create
and myths and prophecies
of clement times
will have been effaced
because
there are no people left

Charles Glass

Palace Hotel, Suleimaniya

Friday, 28 March 2003

The war, such as it is, goes on elsewhere, and there is not much for us to do. We send a short spot to *Good Morning America* on Iraq's Chemchemal evacuation and have lunch at the hotel. Don, Fabrice and Andy are bored. Bruno leaves for Karahanjir, about halfway between Chemchemal and Kirkuk, then aborts the trip. Don and I drive up to the Iraqi National Congress house in Dokan and have dinner at the Ashur Hotel bar with an American colonel from the US embassy in Cairo, Ted Seel, and some INC people, including Francis Brooks. Ted knows Jim Ritchie, another army colonel who was defense attaché in Beirut in 1987 and whom I liked. When Ritchie was a major he told young Lieutenant Seel to move to the Middle East for an interesting life. (Ritchie told me many years later that the Middle East was a graveyard for military and diplomatic careers. Ted agrees.) We drink a lot before and during dinner. When the food is cleared away, Ted and Francis open up.

Don and Ted talk about Vietnam, where Don took some of his most memorable photographs and where Ted did two one-year tours. Ted served in what the army called 'helicopter observation'. He flew as close to the ground as *this*, he says, his hand gliding a foot above a bowl of pistachios on the table. I do not write while he speaks, but make notes later in my room. This paraphrases his words:

'And I could see them, just like I see you,' he says, looking at the INC's Nabil Musawi opposite. 'Observation? It was assassination. You get used to it. We just shot them at close range. I didn't care anymore. Then I asked myself, was there anyone I would not kill?' He stops speaking, and we wait for the answer. I think he will swallow more whisky – he is already through half a bottle of Teacher's – but he doesn't. He says: 'No.'

Then he says he never took R&R. Why not? When he arrived in the country, his platoon lieutenant took R&R with his wife in Hawaii. When he came back, he shot himself. Then two other guys in his unit went on R&R. They came back, took more drugs and had nervous breakdowns. So, Ted stayed in Vietnam for the full year, both times. He was a private first class for a long time – too long, he says. Then he worked up the ranks. He says that, in his unit of assassins, one was an opium addict, two were homicidal maniacs and one was an alcoholic. (I guess Ted could have been the alcoholic, but I might be wrong. He drinks a lot, but holds his liquor.) At the end of his first tour, he boarded a military transport for the States. He had a window seat and looked out at Vietnam. Then he thought about all the people he shot. Suddenly, he says, the tears came. He hid his face, pressing it into the window. He looked at the guy next to him, hoping he had not noticed his tears; the guy didn't see anything – he was crying, too. Ted looked around the plane, he says, and everyone was crying. He was nineteen.

That was in the late 1960s, when John Wayne made the movie *The Green Berets*. At sixteen, I worked on that film part-time as Wayne's driver. One of the technical advisors, who I more or less hero-worshipped, was a Special Forces major named Jerry Dodds. One night after filming at Warner Brothers, I asked Dodds about Vietnam. He was drunk, and grabbed me by the shirt. I remember him saying, 'You don't know what we're doing there. I kill people. I would kill anyone. I would kill your father if they told me to. I would kill you.' He was shaking. Because I was a young patriot who still believed the war was right, I tried to ignore what he said. That was before I read about the murderous Phoenix Program and Operation Speedy Express.

Francis and Ted talk about the American Civil War. Ted's grandfather fought for the Confederacy and killed himself after the war. Francis's people also fought for the rebels, although one ancestor was an abolitionist. My great-grandfather was in the Union Army. We argue about that war, 150 years later, in the midst of a war in Iraq, still getting angry about it; we three Americans are colonizing the table, all at one end, while the Iraqis listen from the other.

Ted and his wife have six children. Their two sons were in the army, but left. One son is doing well as a civilian. The older boy, thirty-one, attempted suicide. Ted is not sympathetic and told his son so. If you kill yourself, he says he warned the boy,

I won't feel guilty. Perhaps that was Ted's way of preventing another attempt. I want to tell Ted my mother killed herself, that you cannot stop it. It's like an incurable disease, a cancer, that eats you up. But the conversation takes another turn. We drink more. Then Francis talks about Saddam.

He says he would support the elimination of Saddam, even if every single Iraqi were killed in the process. I ask him to repeat what he said, and he does. He means it. 'I'm coming from a place different from you,' he says in that soft Southern drawl that you hear from preachers and conmen. 'I believe in good and evil. That man is absolute evil and must be destroyed.' That Virginian voice honed itself for twelve years in Decatur, an Atlanta suburb, and mellowed in the corridors of Washington. But I don't know where the ideas come from. He says he believes in Jesus, resurrection and eternity. If all the Iraqis die, he says, they will live in eternity. But the 'human Satan' must go, no matter what. Ted tells Francis he knows where he comes from, but he cannot go as far.

Ted knows more about killing than Francis does.

Arnold Wesker

Abuse Not Words

Abuse not words they will betray.

Treacherous are they
Who hurl their tired jargon into winds
For winning praise and following.

Abuse not words to catch with vulgar spites
The sad and vulnerable who
Fed on sour delights
Acquire crude crafts,
Harangue and scowl
Leaving others to mother
And heal bleak language
Lethal cant
Has raped and sapped and fouled.

Abuse not words.

Abused they'll glow
Ephemerally then go
Blown with all who followed you.
Crippled language has no power
Blood may flow, true
But will not flower
Brothers. Momentary militants
Perhaps, whose words can dip
No deeper than their pocket's discontent
The cheap linguistic cuts you take
Build no utopian avenues but soon unmake
Where once stood
Your lovely dreams of brotherhood.

Abuse not words.

All you found
Will be too easily brought down.
Words bruised rebound
Boomerang, flounder
Curse those who bruised them, stand
No longer than tomorrow's anger.

Would you weary energies
Burn out belief
Turn all you believed to disbelief
Affront your souls with bored liturgies?
What you fought lovingly to use

Do not abuse.
Abused words will explode
Revengefully when sent
For evidence and argument.
Those you harangue are not detained
Beyond intoxicated moment.

Be warned!
What is trifled with brings grief
Disappointment in old age.
The warm heart aches it aches
With cold ill-use
Shrill and chilled
Page after page after page.

Aamer Hussein

The Book of Maryam

It was the shortest day of the year. Poets, writers and thinkers were to gather to speak about the state of the world at a symposium about the role of the writer in troubled times. It was only a few nights before Christmas and they'd found it hard to book a room at the university as the holidays had already begun. And to make things more difficult, the day they'd chosen was a Friday.

Murad had found out from a mail she'd sent him only a few days before that his friend Tahira, the celebrated and controversial poet from Karachi, would be stopping over on her way back from New York. He thought she'd be a perfect late addition to their gathering. He elected himself as reception committee and went off to Heathrow to pick her up on Thursday evening. But though he waited several hours she didn't appear. When he got home there was no message from her.

They made an announcement at the start of the symposium the next morning that Tahira would be reading at the end of the day. Before midday she called on Ayla's mobile to tell them she'd arrived. Should she take the tube from Heathrow? They told her to get a taxi and they'd pay at their end. She arrived forty minutes later, harassed and hungry, and the taxi driver wanted fifty pounds. Ayla and Murad had been waiting for her on the stairs. Luckily, they had just about that much between them in their wallets.

They took Tahira to lunch at the nearby Italian sandwich bar, which was the only place open, and watched her eat a heaped plate of pasta with pesto and chicken. It was two-thirty and the symposium was in progress. They'd have to miss a couple of presentations.

'They stopped me on my way out of New York,' Tahira told them. 'Though my entry papers should have been in order and I'd had no trouble getting in even with my Pakistani passport, they said they had no record of my arrival three weeks before – and I didn't have my letter of invitation any more, I'd handed it over to immigration. I'm not even going to tell you what they put me through for three hours, it's too tiring. Anyway, it turned out that I'd come in at the other airport and that was part of the problem. So I missed my flight and had to pay a cancellation fee …'

The overcrowded classroom was painted white and lit with bluish neon. The only windows were very, very high and all you could see through them were squares of black. It was four by the time Tahira took her place. Her voice was slightly hoarse, and strong. She read an old poem, then a new one. Silence settled, punctuated only by applause, both surprisingly resonant in the rectangular, nakedly lit room.

Tahira read two more pieces: difficult to say if you could call them poems. One was about the wife of a policeman who was arrested for accepting a tiny bribe; to feed herself and their children, she'd taken part in a homemade porn video and been arrested too. The kids took to the street. The second was about two girls: one raped by Indian soldiers on a train while the staff looked on and cheered, the other, a twelve-year-old, raped by American soldiers in Taiwan. Tahira's readings had no obvious relevance to the war to come and Murad could sense some discomfort, before a heckler with a black beard called out, 'This is reportage, journalism, agitprop – not art. What does it have to do with art or peace or poetry or the war to come?'

She ignored the heckler and went on with her reading. Her next piece was about a poet who was also a minor bureaucrat until he earned the disfavour of the current regime, how he was looked after first by the local prostitutes' union and then given a job in a leading businessman's office where he was led to a desk and told his task was merely to sit down and write. Though the protagonist was male, Murad recognized the latter anecdote as autobiographical. Then a very fat man who looked like a fish that had been kept in a can for twenty years walked in. He wore a blue uniform with rows of buttons and was sweating heavily. He must have been some sort of janitor. He was shouting at them all: probably reminding everyone that their time in the building was over, which was fair enough, but the only words people could hear were 'fuck, fuck, fuck', and then the audience's interventions, about art and freedom and racism and police states. Tahira went on reading during the interruptions; she abruptly stopped when the fat man walked right up to her, left the platform and came down to the audience to grab Murad's arm. He led her out of the room, apologizing.

'Not your fault,' she said.

They had to walk down a long corridor, lined on one side with what seemed like miles of plate glass. Outside it was blind-dark though it was only about five o'clock. Inside the blue lights were switching off one by one. But blue glares lit them up from the outside. No one said very much. Two of the postgraduate students and maybe four or five others from the English department had hung on while the others dispersed. They were leading Tahira and her friends to a place where they could have a drink and maybe even a sandwich as Ayla and Murad hadn't eaten. The students did all the talking.

They got to a cavernous, brightly lit refectory, a place of steel, chrome and perspex. Tables swam in the light like mushrooms. They sat down. Even before they'd got their drinks an Indian man was asking Tahira why she'd targeted Indian soldiers in her poem when it was, after all, Pakistan that was ruled by a military dictator. Tahira didn't reply; she just looked tired. So Ayla asked, probably to rescue the situation, 'Tell us. What are you working on now?'

'A translation into Urdu,' Tahira replied. 'Of my favourite poem. My version of it's called 'The Book of Maryam.''

'We didn't really get to hear enough of you,' Ayla said. 'That bloody interruption. Could you read us a few passages?'

Tahira started, without hesitation, her voice very soft and pure, like a hymn or a requiem. '*How can I have a son*,' she said, *'when no man has touched me ... nor am I sinful?'*

But Oliver the redhead, who'd been poet-in-residence at the college that term, was also talking in a loud, flat voice. 'I had a dream last night,' he said. 'I dreamed I'd been invited to read in a country where everybody wore a veil and bowed a lot and talked about a Great Leader.'

'Oh, yes,' said Violet, the Critical Theory person, in her Yorkshire voice. Tahira was still reading quietly:

> *The birth pangs led her to the trunk of a date-palm tree.*
> *'Would that I had died before this,' she said,*
> *'and become a thing forgotten, unremembered.'*

'They took me to a theatre much bigger than an ordinary theatre,' Oliver went on. 'I was meant to read there but when I went to the stage, which was three times the size of an ordinary stage, it was full of dancers crowding around me. They were dressed in flowing robes of very bright colours, primary colours, purple and red and blue. They had veils on. Masks and half-veils and netted veils.'

'Oh, yes,' said Vi.

Tahira had stopped her recitation. She had the same bewildered expression in her eyes as when the fat man had interrupted her reading. She had a fixed half-smile on her mouth.

'They flooded the stage,' Oliver said, 'and then they were waving banners. Banners with pictures on them and praise of the Great Leader. They had bells on, lots of bells, on the edges of their banners, their robes, on their wrists, on their ankles. They went jingle jingle jingle, they went ching ching ching, they went ...'

'Oh, yes,' said Vi.

Tahira was still silent, looking up, looking down, smiling slightly.

'And then?'

'Then I woke up.'

'But could you see the Leader's face? Saddam, I suppose?'

'Oh, no,' Oliver said. 'The Leader was veiled.'

Tahira and Ayla were nudging each other and laughing.

'Masters of the Universe,' Ayla said, before Tahira took up her recitation again:

> *Then a voice called to her from below:*
> *'Grieve not;*
> *your Lord has made a rivulet gush forth right below*
> *you.*
> *Shake the trunk of the date-palm tree*
> *and it will drop ripe dates for you.*
> *Eat and drink, and be at peace.'*

Tahira paused. There was silence for a moment. Then all the lights went out.

Zapiro
Untitled

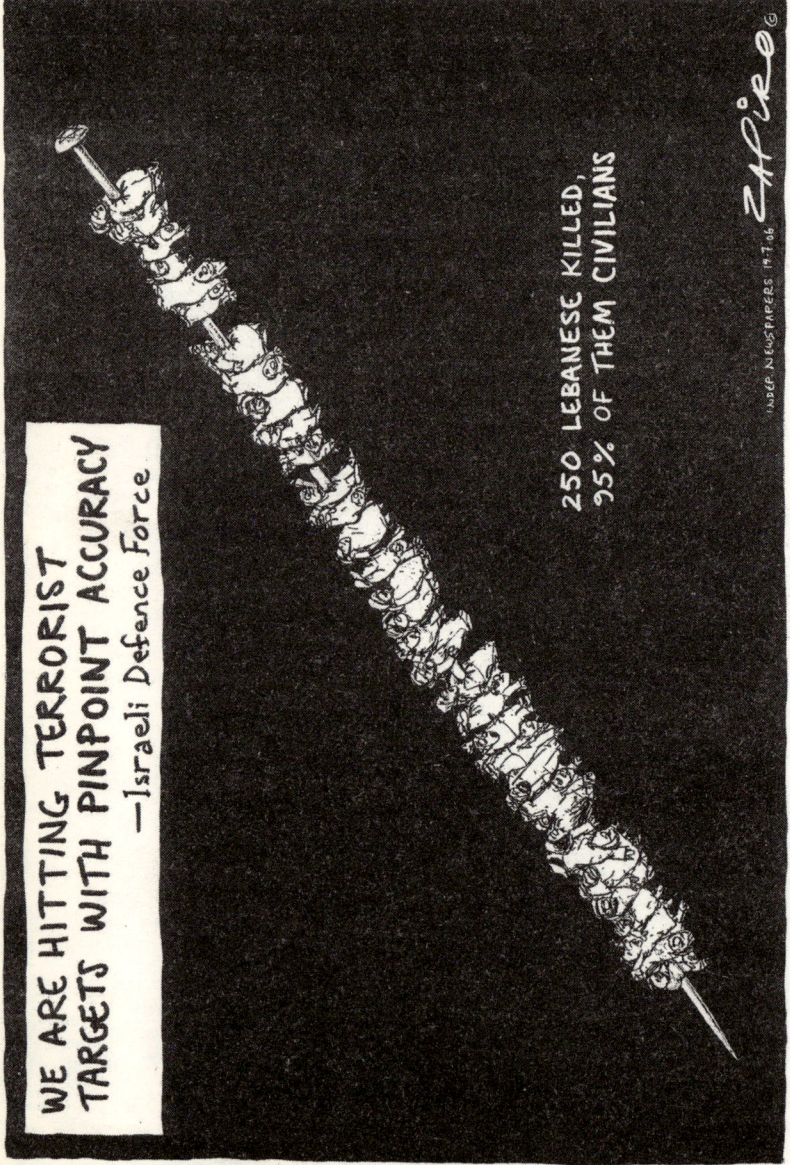

Rebecca O'Connor

Trench

Why kill a man?

    To make him dead.

And what if he has nine lives?

    Then try and try again.

True, God loves a trier
    … but what if I die trying?

Then you're better off dead.

Adrian Mitchell

The Doorbell

I was in bed, the silvery light of dawn
blessing our quiet suburban street,
when the window darkened,
and the doorbell rang.

Pushed my face deep in the pillow,
but the doorbell kept ringing
and there was another sound,
like the crying of a siren,
so I slopped downstairs
unbolted, unlocked, unchained
and opened the front door.

There, on the doorstep, stood the War.
It filled my front garden,
filled the entire street
and blotted out the sky.
It was human and monstrous,
shapeless, enormous,

with torn and poisoned skin which bled
streams of yellow, red and black.

The War had many millions of heads
both dead and half-alive,
some moaning, some screaming,
some whispering,
in every language known on earth,
goodbye, my love.

The War had many millions of eyes
and all wept tears of molten steel.
Then the War spoke to me
in a voice of bombs and gunfire:
I am your War.
Can I come in?

Lara Frankena

An Old Couple

He can't sleep unless the window is open.

It has something to do with the war,
a burning house.
Maybe there was a child.

She waits until his body jerks
involuntarily and sleep seizes him.
Then she rises to close the window.

She can't stand the noise from the street,
and has never felt safe with the window open.

Carmen Callil

Lebanese Washing Stories

My Lebanese grandfather was a Maronite, from the mountain village of Bsharri, high up near the Cedars of Lebanon. Butros Kahlil Fakhry became Peter Callil when he arrived in Australia, according to some records in 1876, the first Lebanese person to go there. Other records say he arrived in 1881. As he was born in 1863 and thirteen seems a bit young to have sailed in the bottom of a boat to the other side of the world, 1881 seems right, but who knows? He left a tiny country of two million people, only 125 miles long, and was dumped in Melbourne, then a city of half-a-million inhabitants, speaking no English and thinking he was elsewhere anyway. My grandfather had no intention of going to Australia. He wanted to go to America – the United States – where all emigrants wanted to go, or to South America, where there were already others from Bsharri. He was taken to Melbourne, willy nilly; my Last Uncle told me that these unscrupulous sea captains would dump the migrant in Lisbon, or some miscellaneous port, 'Here you are, this is America.' Another trick was to take the hapless migrant to the farthest and costliest place. This was Australia or New Zealand, where many more of the clan settled in the 1890s. There are accounts of Lebanese living in Australia for years before they realised they were not in 'Al-Na-Yurk' (New York).

My grandfather went back to the Lebanon for a wife, my formidable grandmother. They had seven children all born in Australia, five boys and two girls, of whom my Aunt Mary was the elder. My father, the second youngest, died young, and so the remaining siblings loomed large in our childhood. Most of the family lived near my Lebanese grandparents. This was because my grandparents and their children wanted it like this, but also because my grandparents bought their children houses within shouting distance of the family home. In Mary's case though, it was a measure of her lack of favour that she lived at least two suburbs away. I often encountered her on the tram home from the university or school and I learned to hide to avoid the embarrassment of exchanges with her tempestuous person. She was top of the Callil shouting league. Often she would spot me hiding and would shriek through the packed tram, '*There she is, my dead brother's child – and she won't say Hello to her Aunty.*'

Aunt Mary was a rich source of Lebanese washing stories. One day I was passing by her house and saw her munchkin body in the front garden fiercely directing a hose at a fully pegged out rotary line of sodden washing, which also seemed, on closer inspection, to be ramrod stiff with some mysterious substance. She bustled me off to the new washing machine my Number One Uncle had bought for her that day. She had poured the entire contents of three giant packets of Persil into the machine (my family always bought everything in bulk). Lebanese women like to see *suds*, lots of suds. The clothes were rigid with soap, the machine destroyed.

My other aunt Mary, wife to my third uncle, was equally washing orientated. I used to do the family washing on Mondays, in the years when I was at Melbourne University. I hated doing it, and what I didn't bury in the garden I would peg out lickety-split on the rotary line and then retire to my books. This Aunt Mary would turn up and re-peg the whole thing: all *socks* together, all *red socks* together, all *red socks* pegged *in the same direction*, and so on through every colour and item until perfect symmetry was achieved. There are lots of Lebanese washing stories. David Malouf tells of a female relative of his who, whenever he went to stay, woke him up early in the morning by gently rocking him to and fro to ease out the sheet beneath his sleeping body in order to get it into the wash before the day began. Lebanese women are particularly fixated by sheets.

In 1993 I flew to Australia for my Last Uncle's funeral. He died at the age of 91, and almost everyone with a drop of clan blood was there for the funeral. What struck me, looking round the Church, was that everything my grandfather and grandmother set out to do had now been achieved. All the great-grandchildren and cousins, by this time two, three, and four times removed, had bits and pieces of them and of the uncles and aunts bestowed about their persons. There was the curly hair again, there the familiar balding spot; there were the two or three regulation Callil noses, the wheezy chests, and always, for the women, those thunderthigh Mount Lebanon legs. But it was all mixed up with injections from Australians of Irish, Scottish, English, Italian and more various stock. There they all were in their hundreds, clean, bellicose, and flourishing. For those who left the Mountain a hundred years before everything was just as it should be.

Toby Litt

Dialogues

Dialogue I

Grant me the soul – what then?
Speak as essence, badly; speak,
predictably, as putrescence. No.
So you refuse? Then grant me anything
essential at all. I'll take, I'll take
beauty, and an improvement towards
it, line by line. Even philosophy
admits the seventh draft to be
better than the first. No, you say, not
better – and certainly not more
beautiful. Then at least leave me perception;
each eye to have its hole, seeing
outwardly. Or less even than that:
direction, not place, point or origin.
Grant me the length of the line,
sideways.

Then no again.
No repeatedly and without anger.

I understand – I take your
refusal to be absolute. And that
I will take; there I will start; this I will say.

Dialogue II

'Essence is stasis-bang! – stasis plus
effort times pretence.' This
is what you say (to me) – apart
from bang! which you think but
do not say, although you want to;
even more than pretence. 'Wow-
fuck,' I reply, intellectually exhausted.
'Between now and tomorrow's death
I have decisions.' 'Everyone does.'
'Everyone doesn't make them, because
everyone doesn't realise.' 'People
are better at being people than intellectuals
give them credit for.' 'I admit
that.' 'Then act as if you did.'
Speechless, I continue to the issue.

Hoda Barakat

Viva La Diva

How small this corpse is … I thought he was taller and bigger …

My dad used to stare at my suitcase and then look at me: *can you carry it?* A forty-kilo suitcase, and me twenty-five!!

Of course I can carry it.

Do you need help?

NO, I can carry the biggest suitcase in the world if you keep looking at me like that.

Because of those eyes, I can carry the biggest suitcase. I will be the winner; the world turns around according to me, all of it according to me, till I die … or till you die.

Since you are dead I can go wherever I want, Canada, China, or Congo, it doesn't matter.

I feel as if something has broken inside my head and my chest; maybe every time a loved one abandons us, the wire connecting us explodes.

As if one is liberated by pain and suffering … but one *is* liberated when loved ones are gone. *Ooof. Bye, bye, ma'l salameh.* Every man I loved left me agonizing in pain. I cry. I tear out my hair, saying *I don't want to live anymore, enough.* I cry. I tear my hair. Look how I became alone, by myself. How my body is getting older, and uglier. I used to be very pretty but now I will never be the same again. How? How? What a pity … But inside my tiny ripped mouth I feel the taste of Turkish delight. Not a very strong taste, but sugary, and nice … I feel it like a sweet poison or like a warm wine running in my veins. *Ah* … by myself, I am free, it doesn't matter if the phone rings or not. I don't want to wear make-up, or take a shower. I don't want to see anybody or be seen by anybody. I want to get naked and walk madly in the house by myself; I don't want to know which day it is tomorrow: Saturday, Thursday …

And I don't want to sing anymore.

(She stands up and acts the character of Maria Callas)

I want to punish the universe; I will not let them hear the voice of Maria Callas. God graced the universe with my voice, but I will deny them this, without saying – nor anybody knowing.

I told the media: I am a phenomenon, true, but life is short and I might die soon. (In a fake tone.) And all these generations, these youngsters … there is a lot of talent. It is my duty to teach and guide them.

All the people attending the master-class shouted *bravo, bravo Maria!* She is justified in being nervous, because she is serious, and she wants to convey her knowledge and experience, *bravo, wonderful, fascinating … Allah Akabar.*

I lost my voice at sixty-five, and nobody knows.

But there was somebody who understood me, like a magician. He said: Maria you don't want to sing anymore, neither do I want you to. I want you to act in my film. I have been looking for years for a woman to play Medea; Maria you are Medea.

Tell me again: Maria, you are Medea, you are Medea.

How Pasolini witnessed my suffering, my jealousy, my overwhelming desire to kill!

(*Playing the role of Medea*)

How did he see the fire burning inside me? The horrible red dreams, which cannot be seen by the man I loved and chased in the wilderness. In every place I go, walking behind him I leave mutilated bodies. The last thing the Corinthian king said: listen, my daughter is very pretty, marry her, and you will get the throne, you will be the king of my country.

Like the moon, Caruso. I am not pretty and I am getting old; left without children, barren ...

And like the moon, Caruso, I look to the sky, sighing and breathing I see a hundred moons, a thousand Carusos. Oh my God, where are you following me to?

(*Returns to role of Maria Callas*)

Aristotle didn't give me a chance, they didn't give me a chance;

the last thing left for me is pity. You used to cheat on me with other women, lie to me, make an effort at least, don't let me find out, remember me ...

His photos with other women are scattered all over the newspapers.

I kept loving him, but he leaves me
I love him but he leaves me
I love him but he leaves me
He leaves me but I love him.

He doesn't care, because I threaten and get angry with him, but when he calls me, I go back to him with my peevish disregard for his happiness, I spoil it with exasperation, thinking myself strong and able to punish him ... this is wrong.

When I became weak, he felt sorry for me. He said: How beautiful you are, you are greater and more important than me. The whole world will kneel in front of you, Maria how beautiful you are ...

Do you think he noticed that I quit singing? Or maybe he thought I was pampering myself.

Look how the idiot talks to me (*how beautiful you are*)

Pretty? Because I became invulnerable like those pretty women?

Other women are described as beautiful ... Do I need to be more beautiful?

Oh ... the other women ... Every time he cheats I discover it, because it is impossible not to find out – because he wants me to find out. He gives me jewelry to make me look pretty, or to cover my ugliness. Every time he sleeps with one of the 'others' he gives me a ring, a bracelet, a necklace.

He kept sleeping with the pretty 'others' and giving me necklaces until I was strangled; gave me such loads of necklaces that I lost my voice. On the evening of August the fourth, I was wearing one of these necklaces. I retired halfway through the concert. People said: *she refused to finish the concert because she is a diva*. But it was because of the necklace, which strangled the voice in my neck.

There is a special kind of bird in a forest in Brazil. The scientist discovered that their singing is very peculiar, their melodies are so complex, some of them reach the level of symphonies. Although there are huge numbers of these birds in a particular spot in the forest, the male recognizes the female by her distinguished song. He answers her back using the right notes to complete her melody. The scientist claims that by using this form of communication, they each develop their own special melody. Usually these birds live as couples and keep using the same notes, and the same special melodies for the rest of their lives. But if one bird loses his/her partner, it keeps repeating the melody, waiting for the other partner to complete it. The coherent structure of the melody will collapse only in two cases: when the bird loses his/her partner; or when the scientists remove the bird from the forest.

The melody falls apart as well when they call the forest but the forest doesn't reply.

The notes fall apart every time I call the country, my country, but the country doesn't reply.

I want to leave this country

(She goes back to the suitcase, fills it with stuff).

Translated by Hassan Ramadan

Mahmud Darwish

Diaries

The Girl/The Scream

On the seashore is a girl, and the girl has a family
And the family has a house. And the house has two windows
and a door
And in the sea is a warship having fun catching promenaders
On the seashore: four, five, seven
Fall down on the sand. And the girl is saved a little
Because a hazy hand
A divine hand of some sort helps her. She calls out: Father
Father! Let's go home, the sea is not for people like us!
Her father doesn't answer her, laid out on his shadow
Windward of the sunset
Blood in the palm trees, blood in the clouds
Her voice carries her higher and further than
The seashore. She screams at night over the land
Her voice echoes once
She becomes the endless scream of breaking news
Which was no longer breaking news when

The aircraft returned to bomb a house with two windows and a door!

Green Flies

The scene is the same as ever. Summer and sweat. And an invisible fantasy beyond the horizon. And today is better than tomorrow. But the dead are what's new. They're born every day and when they're trying to sleep death takes them away from their drowsing to a dreamless sleep. It's not worth counting them. None of them asks for help from anyone. Voices look for words in the open country, and the echo comes back clearly, woundingly: 'There's nobody here'. But there's somebody who says: 'It's the killer's right to defend the killer instinct,' while the dead say belatedly: 'It's the victim's right to defend his right to scream.' The call to prayer rises to accompany the indistinguishable funerals: coffins hastily raised in the air, hastily buried – no time to carry out the rites, more dead are arriving at speed from other raids, individually or in groups – or a whole family with no orphans or grieving parents left behind. The sky is leaden grey and the sea blue grey, but the colour of blood is hidden from the camera by swarms of green flies.

A Prose Poem

An autumnal summer on the hills like a prose poem. The breeze is a gentle rhythm I feel but do not hear in the modesty of the low trees, and the yellowish plants are peeling images, and eloquence provokes similes with its sly verbs. The only celebration on these mountain paths is provided by the lively sparrows, whose activity veers between sense and nonsense. Nature is a body divesting itself of trivial adornment until the figs, grapes and pomegranates ripen and the rain awakens forgotten desires. 'If it were not for my mysterious need for poetry, I wouldn't need anything,' says the poet whose ardour has waned so his mistakes have grown less. He walks because the doctors have advised him to walk with no particular goal, to train the heart in the indifference which is necessary for good health. Any idea that occurs to him will be purely gratuitous. The summer only rarely lends itself to verse. The summer is a prose poem which takes no interest in the eagles circling high above.

If Only I were a Stone
I would yearn for nothing
No yesterday passing, no tomorrow to come
And my present neither advancing nor retreating
Nothing happening to me!
If only I were a stone – I said – Oh if only I were
Some stone so that water would burnish me
Green, yellow – I would be placed in a room
Like a sculpture, or exercises in sculpture
Or material for the eruption of the necessary
From the folly of the unnecessary
If only I were a stone
So that I could yearn for something!

Beyond Identification

I sit in front of the television, since I can't do anything else.

There, in front of the television, I discover my feelings. I see what's happening to me. Smoke is rising from me and I reach out my severed hand to pick up my scattered limbs from many bodies, and I don't find them but I don't run away from them because pain has such an attraction. I am besieged by land and air and sea and language. The last aircraft has taken off from Beirut airport and put me in front of the television to see the rest of my death with millions of other viewers. Nothing proves that I exist when I think, as Descartes says, but rather when I am offered up in sacrifice, now, in Lebanon. I enter the television, I and the beast. I know the beast is stronger than me in the struggle, with his aircraft and his pilot. But I became addicted, perhaps more than I should have done, to the heroism of the metaphor: the beast swallowed me, but did not digest me. I emerged unscathed more than once. My soul, confused in the belly of the beast, inhabited another body, lighter and stronger. But now I don't know where I am: in front of the television or inside it. Whereas I can see my heart rolling like a pine cone from a Lebanese mountain to Gaza!

The Enemy

I was there a month ago. I was there a year ago. I was always there as if I was never anywhere else. In 1982 the same thing happened to us as is happening now. We were besieged and killed and fought against the hell we encountered. The casualties/ martyrs don't resemble one another. Each of them has a distinctive physique and distinctive features, different eyes and a different name and age. But the killers are the ones who all look the same. They are one being, distributed over different pieces of machinery, pressing electronic buttons, killing and vanishing. He sees us and we don't see him, not because he's a ghost but because he's a steel mask on an idea – he is featureless, eyeless, ageless and nameless. It is he who has chosen to have a single name: the enemy.

Nero

What's going on in Nero's mind as he watches Lebanon burn? His eyes wander ecstatically and he walks like someone dancing at a wedding: this madness is my madness, I know best, so let them set light to everything outside my control – and the children have to learn to behave themselves and stop shouting when I'm playing my tunes!

And what's going on in Nero's mind as he watches Iraq burn? Does it please him that he awakens a memory in the forests of history which preserves his name as an enemy of Hamurabbi and Gilgamesh and Abu Nuwas: my law is the mother of all laws, and the flower of eternity grows in my fields, and poetry, what does that mean?

And what goes on in Nero's mind as he watches Palestine burn? Does it delight him that his name is recorded in the roll of prophets as a prophet that nobody's ever believed in before? As a prophet of killing whom God entrusted with correcting the countless mistakes in the heavenly books: 'I too am God's mouthpiece'!

And what goes on in Nero's mind as he watches the world burn? 'I am master of the day of judgement.' Then he orders the camera to stop rolling, because he doesn't want anyone to see the fire burning his fingers at the end of this long American movie!

The Forest

I couldn't hear my voice in the forest, even if
The forest were free of the beast's hunger … and the army
Defeated or victorious, there's no difference, had returned over
The severed limbs of the unknown dead to the barracks or
The throne/
And I couldn't hear my voice in the forest, even if
The wind carried it to me, and said to me:
'Here's your voice' … I couldn't hear it/
I couldn't hear my voice in the forest even if
The wolf stood on his hind legs and clapped his hands
At me: 'I can hear your voice, so give me your orders!'/
And I would say: The forest is not in the forest,
Wolf, my son, my son!/
I couldn't hear my voice unless
The forest were free of me, and I were free of
The silence of the forest.

Doves

A flight of doves scatters suddenly from a break in the smoke, shining like a gleam of heavenly peace, circling between the grey and the fragments of blue above a city of rubble and reminding us that beauty still exists and that non-existence is not making complete fools of us since it promises us, or we think it does, a revelation of how it is different from nothingness. In war none of us feels that he is dead if he feels pain. Death pre-empts pain, pain is the one blessing in war. It moves from quarter to quarter bringing a stay of execution. And if someone is befriended by luck he forgets his long-term plans and waits for the non-existent that already exists circling in a flight of doves. I see many doves in the skies of Lebanon playing with the smoke that rises from the nothingness.

The House as Casualty

In one minute the entire life of a house is ended. The house as casualty is also mass murder even if it is empty of its inhabitants. A mass grave of raw materials intended to build a structure with meaning, or a poem with no importance in time of war. The house as casualty is the severance of things from their relationships and from the names of feelings, and from the need of tragedy to direct its eloquence at seeing into the life of the object. In every object there is a being in pain ... a memory of fingers, of a smell, of an image. And houses are killed just like their inhabitants. And the memory of objects is killed: stone, wood, glass, iron, cement are scattered in broken fragments like living beings. And cotton, silk, linen, papers, books torn to pieces like proscribed words. Plates, spoons, toys, records, water taps, pipes, door handles, the fridge, the washing machine, flower vases, jars of olives and pickles, tinned food all break just like their owners. Salt, sugar, spices, boxes of matches, pills, contraceptives are crushed to pieces / and antidepressants, strings of garlic, onions, tomatoes, dried okra, rice and lentils, just like their owners. Rent agreements, marriage documents, birth certificates, water and electricity bills, identity cards, passports, love letters are torn in shreds like their owners' hearts. Photographs, toothbrushes, combs, cosmetics, shoes, underwear, sheets, towels like family secrets broadcast aloud in the devastation. All these things are a memory of the people who no longer have them and of the objects that no longer have the people ... destroyed in one minute. Our things die like us, but they aren't buried with us.

The Cunning of the Metaphor

As a metaphor I say: I was victorious
As a metaphor I say: I lost ...
And a very deep valley lies before me
And I lie in what remains of the holm oak
And there are two olive trees
Surrounding me on three sides
And two birds carry me
To the side which is empty
Of the peak and the abyss
So that I don't say: I was victorious
So that I don't say: I lost the bet

Infiltration Exercise

Today, 26 July, twenty-one casualties/martyrs in Gaza, among them two infants, have managed to pass through the military checkpoints and barbed wire ... and infiltrate the news bulletin. They didn't make any comment as their pain fell from them before they got as far as words. And they didn't disclose their names because these were so poor and ordinary. And they didn't make victory signs to the camera because the camera was crowded with more exciting images. War is excitement, a TV series where each new instalment destroys the previous one and one massacre cancels out another. And when the killing starts happening daily it becomes normal and the dead turn into numbers, death becomes routine and the temperature never goes above the thirties. Routine creates boredom. Boredom distances the viewer from the screen, and puts the correspondent out of a job. When the viewing figures drop the advertisements dry up and the whole industry of producing images goes into recession. Added to that: the shots of Gaza have become familiar and uninspiring. A leaden sky above narrow alleys in camps without sea views. There are no hills there and no landscapes for the viewer to enjoy. Everything is ordinary the killing is ordinary and the funeral is ordinary and the streets are grey. But what is out of the ordinary today is: that twenty-one casualties/martyrs have managed boldly and without guides to infiltrate the news bulletin!

The Mosquito

The mosquito, and I don't know what the masculine form of the word is in Arabic, is more destructive than slander. Not content with sucking your blood, it forces you into a vicious battle. It only visits in darkness like al-Mutanabbi's fever. It buzzes and hums like a warplane which you don't hear until it has hit its target: your blood. You switch on the light to see it and it disappears into some secret corner of the room, then settles on the wall ... safe, peaceful, as if it has surrendered. You try to kill it with one of your shoes, but it dodges you and escapes and reappears with an air of malicious satisfaction. You try again and fail. You curse it loudly and it pays no attention. You negotiate a truce with it in a friendly voice: sleep so that I can sleep! You think you've convinced it and switch off the light and go to sleep. But having sucked most of your blood it starts humming again, threatening a new attack. And forces you into a subsidiary battle with your sweat. You turn on the light again and resist the two of them, the mosquito and the sweat, by reading. But the mosquito lands on the page you are reading, and you say happily to yourself: it's fallen into the trap. And you snap the book shut: I've killed it … I've killed it! And when you open the book to glory in your victory, there's no sign of the mosquito or the words. Your book is blank. The mosquito, and I don't know what the masculine form of the word is in Arabic, is not a metaphor, an allusion or an innuendo. It's an insect which likes your blood. It can smell it from twenty miles away. There's only one way you can bargain with it to make a truce: by changing your blood group.

The Rest of a Life

If someone said to me: 'You're going to die here this evening
So what will you do in the time that remains?'
— I would look at my watch/
I would drink a glass of juice
And nibble an apple
And stare for a long time at an ant that had found her food for
    the day
Then look at my watch/
There is still time for me to shave

And take a long shower/I would have a sudden notion

'One should look nice to write/

So I'll wear something blue'/

I would sit until noon active at my desk

Not seeing a trace of colour in the words

White, white, white ...

I would prepare my last meal

Pour wine in two glasses: for me

And an unexpected guest

Then take a siesta between two dreams/

But the sound of my snoring will wake me ...

Then I would look at my watch:

There is still time to read/

I would read a canto of Dante and half a mu'allaqa

And see how my life goes away from me

Into other people, and not wonder who

Will take its place

– Just like that?

– Just like that

– Then what?

– I would comb my hair, and throw the poem ...

This poem in the rubbish bin

Put on my newest shirt from Italy

Say my final farewell to myself with a backing of Spanish violins

Then walk to the graveyard!

Qana

Translated by Catherine Cobham

Margaret Drabble

Lebanon

Once upon a time, about fifty years ago, I worked as an au pair girl for three months with a French Protestant Marxist family. The parents were intellectuals and teachers of English, and their children were numerous and most of the time delightful. I learned a great deal from that family. I learned some French, which was the ostensible purpose of my visit, but I also learned about French cooking and French communism. It was a period of hard work, both physical and mental, and I benefited from it greatly.

One of the more unexpected benefits has been my friendship with the Lebanese writer, Rachid El-Daïf, whom I met through the oldest daughter of this French family. She in turn, in the 1970s, came to stay with me in London as an au pair for my children, and later she sent to us her friend (and future husband) Rachid, who had been studying for his doctorate at the Sorbonne in Paris. He came to London in part because he was taking refuge from the Lebanese civil war, which broke out in 1975, and he stayed with me for some weeks. I think this must have been in 1976, but I cannot be sure of the dates. Again, this was a period of intense learning for me. Rachid's

English was not as good as it is now (and indeed I now think he had an objection to the English language, which represented American imperialism). My schoolgirl French had fallen into neglect, but we talked in French, which was difficult for me, and I am not sure that I always understood him correctly. But we tried hard to communicate, and I have vivid memories of our long conversations, and of his attempts to teach me about the politics of the Middle East. Although he came from a Maronite Christian family, he was then a Marxist, and his line on events was Marxist and pro-Muslim. He had a complex multiple identity, a theme about which he has written much.

We talked, about the Jews and the Arabs, about the Soviet Union, about Israel, about the CIA and the PLO, about Hollywood distortions of American life and American perceptions of Arab culture. My first husband is Jewish, and I was much more familiar with generally received liberal Jewish views on the Middle East: it was a salutary shock to me to hear another point of view presented and argued so forcefully. I think we both helped to educate one another. He asked me once why the 'Royal Free Hospital' down the road from our house was called 'Free', and I well remember how I was able to boast that all the hospitals in England were free. He was astonished.

Eventually Rachid returned to the Lebanon, to take up his career of teaching Arabic language and literature at the Lebanese University in Beirut. But the political situation there went from bad to worse. Communications with the outside world were almost non-existent, and the newsreels showed daily and appalling carnage. I thought of him frequently, because he had by chance become my point of emotional and personal contact with a disastrous sequence of events. I learned that he was living in West Beirut, where he had been seriously injured in a car bomb explosion, but had survived. I wondered what he thought about the way the war was going, and whether his politics had changed. (They had.)

I can't remember how we made contact again. News about him gradually began to filter through. I learned that he published a volume of poems in 1979, and then several novels, some of which were translated from Arabic into French, and some, a little later, into English and other languages. I read what I could of his fiction, which gives a vivid, haunting picture of basic survival in a Kafkaesque world of siege, road blocks, identity checks, dirt and poverty. At least, I thought, he was making good use of his experiences.

Slowly, slowly, in the 1990s, after the fifteen years of war ended, life in the Lebanon began to improve, and so did communications. Telephone lines were restored, and the internet became accessible. Rachid, always up with the new technology when given a chance, was able to assure me by email that life was much better, that his prospects were good. He came to Europe, and we met and exchanged literary and family news. His son Unsi, continuing the tradition of exchange, came to stay with friends of mine to learn some English. (My son Joe, meanwhile, had been to work on a kibbutz near the Golan Heights in 1985.) I felt such pleasure for Rachid, and through him for the whole country, which was returning to normal life and prosperity, and becoming once more part of the international community.

Rachid was free to travel abroad, and tourism in his homeland was flourishing. He had become a man of the world, invited to conferences. In September 2001 he was scheduled to speak in Geneva, under the auspices of UNCTAD (United Nations Conference on Trade and Development): he prepared a paper on the values of literature and politics, the failure of political analysis, the meaning of war, the impulses that drive suicide bombers, and the question of Arab identity. He described his country as a beautiful land, 'ruined by the sport of nations'. He delivered this powerful and personal address two days before the Twin Towers collapsed. Rachid has always lived close to history.

I used to dream idly that maybe I would go one day to see him in his native village in Zgharta in the north. I have in my head a child's picture book image of this village, composed of scraps of poems and conversations, in which I see Rachid as a little boy in a huge bed with his six brothers and his little sister, all in a row under one woven coverlet, with their mother in the middle, smiling proudly at her brood. Outside I can see the snowy mountains and the wooded slopes and the biblical cedars of Lebanon, and indoors on little tables are placed dishes of dates and figs, and the bowls of goat yoghurt which Rachid loved so much. It's a simple, once-upon-a-time fairy story picture of happiness and plenty, of childhood as it ought to be. In his novel, *Dear Mr Kawabata* (1995; English version, 1999), he asks the reader, 'Have you ever tasted the milk of goats, heated with a little mint from a garden warmed by the sun in front of the door, and watered from a nearby spring, water from a spring that is cool even in the heat of summer? I used to feel that when I drink goat's milk I am at peace with life ...'

I will never go to the Lebanon and taste the goat's milk. That daydream is over. Once more, the country has been destroyed. Its buildings and its bridges have been reduced to rubble, its fleeing population has been bombed as it tried to escape the attacks, and its children have been buried alive. Its coastline is awash with deadly black seas of oil. Sixteen years of laborious reconstruction have been ferociously crushed. The waste of human life and human effort is appalling. The devastation is unspeakably shocking. So many years of labour have been wantonly undone in three weeks. I never thought I would feel sorry for bricks and mortar and breeze blocks, but I do. They represent the hands and hopes of men.

I see more clearly now why Rachid's novels are full of building sites and bulldozers and construction and deconstruction. That is the history of the region.

His novels of the 1980s and 1990s are eloquent on the theme of destruction and endurance. One of them is called *Techniques de la misère* (1989; Arabic, *Tiqaniyat al-bu's*), a phrase which is hard to translate, and which indeed needs no translation. This novel is about dull, grim, grey day-to-day survival, in a half-ruined city, where life goes on, and the plumber never comes. Everyday objects take on a malign objective obstructive life: taps, cisterns, telephone lines, buckets, candles, the generator, and holes in the road provide occasion for hourly negotiation. You have to learn to deal patiently with these mindless things. Each daily act is a challenge. Rachid, in an interview in 1989, says that 'misery' (or 'poverty', or 'despair') requires skill, or *savoir-faire*: you have to learn how to be miserable, just as you have to learn how to be a carpenter or a stonemason.

And now the Lebanese people will have to learn the art of misery all over again.

All victims, says Rachid El-Daïf, as others have said before him, become executioners. '*Il n'est pas de victime qui ne se transforme en bourreau.*' He has watched the cycle go round once, and now the whole damn thing begins again. I have seen him grow from an intense idealistic thirty-year-old ideologue into a benign man with a sceptical and benevolent smile. It is good that he is there to bear witness, but he must have wished that he would not be called once more to bear witness to these violent acts of anger and hatred and folly and revenge.

Clare Pollard

The Bad News

This evening the sickle of the wind felled a city.
This evening girls slid like new calves to the sand,
eyes webs for flies, tongues thick with thirst's flavour.
This evening ancient vessels went jag-toothed dancing
at the knotty feet of looters, whilst women bayed
like wolves to the star in the power cut's dark,
for their youngest, slain by lion-faced men.

This evening, in dark intestines, super bugs
invisibly bred, knitting their message: death, death.
This evening parents pampered their dolled, rouged tots,
and mothers-of-ten sewed themselves to death,
fumble-fingered on mandatory double-shifts.
This evening a whale's gorgeous callused heft
thrashed the harpoon gut-deep, to rot and nothing.

This evening, the children of Africa kinged and scrapped
amongst the ghostly stones of our outdated fridges.
This evening warheads point their noses at us,

like the fragile, curious noses of wet rats,
and men feasted on the belly of a peacekeeper
in groin-damp jungle where the monkeys cry: *oo oo.*
This evening no one cared what we thought.

This evening a man turned the key of his ignition
and drove 'For the hell of it' through golden hits and suburbs,
and a sea of glass mingled with oil and fire
and seals basked in ineradicable darkness.
This evening politicians plotted profitable slaughter.
This evening a man on a bus opened the gates
to a hundred black horses with manes of flame.

This evening as we waited in the ward for the bad news,
in its faint tang of shit, beside the old man who rocked
and cried out moistly for his 'Mam',
a black alphabet of swallows clouded the low sun,
except I thought that they spelt: death, death,
and I thought that I could hear the whole ill earth tick
closer now, towards the end, into evening.

Alexandre Najjar

Hope

The war that ravaged Lebanon from 1975 to 1990 did not spare a thing: the infrastructure, the economy, national unity, the joy of living ... I remember the horrific nights lit by fire, the deafening din of shelling, the whistling of the militiamen's bullets; I recall the dead transported in bin liners, the injured piled up in ambulances, the refugees sleeping in car parks, the car bombs, the devastated buildings, the shattered windows and the barricades; I can still smell the odour of blood, of powder, of dirt ... And I ask myself how and why I came out of it unharmed, though I guess one is never quite unharmed after such an ordeal.

During the war, my father, by nature an optimist, developed projects for the future, urged his relatives and friends not to abandon ship, convinced that the 'good Lebanese' ought to stick together and not desert their country. To those who came to him to lament the loss of their belongings, he promised better days; to those who felt despondency take over them, he assured the imminent end to the fighting; to those who wished to take the path of exile, he explained that exile was not a remedy, but poison. Was he himself convinced of what he was preaching, or was he bluffing in order to persuade them to stay? He felt, I think, entrusted with a national, almost divine mission to preach hope: people came to see him discouraged, they left confident, with a skip in their step.

One day, when the bombs were raining down, my mother came to find him with a worried look on her face:

'What's wrong?' he asked her.

'I fear protests in front of our house.'

My father frowned, walked towards the window and drew the curtains.

'Protests? Who would want to protest in front of our home?'

My mother shrugged and answered in a deadpan tone: 'All those to whom you gave false hopes, who remained in Lebanon because of you; all those whom you comforted, and who, at this hour, are hiding underground like rats to escape the shelling!'

My father always looked on the bright side, would see that the glass was half-full. He was so optimistic that he had the utmost difficulty in imagining old age or death. At the age of seventy-three he was offended when I classed him in the category of elderly people: 'I am not old,' he corrected me sternly. And when my uncle passed away suddenly, I recall my father full of hope in the car leading us to the hospital, incapable of imagining his brother dead. When we reached the emergency room and my tearful sister told us it was over, he looked lost for a while, with a haggard gaze and pursed lips.

'It's impossible,' he stammered, shaking me like an apple

tree. 'We have to save him, it's impossible!'

'There's nothing we can do, Dad. He's gone.'

'It's impossible,' he repeated. 'It's impossible ...'

Indeed it was possible. Death had taken away my uncle, he who was goodness itself, he who, in a letter sent to Dad, had written these words: 'You are a father to all of us; you are and will always remain our last recourse.'

Another day, during the most critical stage of the war, while we were always in shelters, confined to an obscure and malodorous room, listening to the sound of explosions that were shaking the city above our heads, we saw my father (who was a lawyer) arrive with a candle and a pile of folders.

'What are you doing, Dad?'

'I have these files to finish,' he answered, settling himself in a corner of the shelter.

'What files? The country is ruined. There are neither clients, nor tribunals, nor judges, nor justice ... What's the point?'

My father nodded and said these magnificent words: 'Tomorrow peace will come and I need to be ready.'

Translated by Yasmine Gaspard

Paul Auster

Credo

The infinite

Tiny things. For once merely to breathe
In the light of the infinite

tiny things
that surround us. Or nothing
can escape

the lure of this darkness, the eye
will discover that we are
only what has made us less
than we are. To say nothing. To say:
our very lives

depend on it.

David Medalla
The poet's libation to the moon

About the Contributors

Etel Adnan was born in 1925 in Beirut. She has published more than ten books of poetry and fiction. She lives in California, Paris and Lebanon.

Adonis, born in 1930 in Qassabin, Northern Syria, is one of the Middle East's foremost contemporary poets. He is also a literary critic, translator and editor.

Paul Auster was born in New Jersey in 1947. He is one of America's most highly acclaimed novelists. He is also a poet, translator, editor, scriptwriter and filmmaker.

Hoda Barakat is one of the most original voices in modern Arabic literature. She won the Naguib Mahfouz prize with *The Tiller of Waters*. Her novel *The Stone of Laughter*, which won the al-Naqid prize, was the first Arabic novel to have a gay man as its central character.

John Berger is an art critic, novelist, painter and author. The best-known among his many works include the novel *G.*, which won the Booker Prize, and the introductory essay on art criticism *Ways of Seeing*.

Abbas Beydoun was born in Tyre in Lebanon. He has six collections of poetry and is Cultural Editor of *As-Safir* newspaper in Beirut.

Issa J. Boullata was born in Jerusalem, Palestine, and was Professor of Arabic Literature and Language at McGill University in Montreal. He is the author of numerous books and has translated many Arabic poems into English. He is currently Contributing Editor of *Banipal*.

Raymond Briggs was born in London in 1934, and is one of Britain's most acclaimed children's author-illustrators. He also writes books for adults, such as *When the Wind Blows*, a grim satire on nuclear war.

Carmen Callil was born in Melbourne in 1938. She came to the UK in 1960 and founded Virago Press in 1972. She later became Managing Director of Chatto & Windus and The Hogarth Press. She is the author (with Colm Tóibín) of *The Modern Library: The 200 Best Novels in English since 1950*, and *Bad Faith: A Forgotten History of Family and Fatherland*.

John le Carré was born in 1931. He spent five years in the British Foreign Service. *The Spy Who Came In from the Cold* secured him a worldwide reputation as a novelist. He divides his time between England and the Continent.

Jung Chang is a Chinese-born British writer, best known for her bestselling autobiography *Wild Swans*. Her latest book, which she wrote with Jon Halliday, is *Mao: The Unknown Story*.

Catherine Cobham teaches Arabic at St Andrews University, Scotland and has translated a number of contemporary Arab writers, including Yusuf Idris, Naguib Mahfouz, Hanan al-Shaykh and Fuad al-Takarli.

Hassan Daoud is Chief Editor of *Nawafez* (Windows), the cultural supplement for *Al Mustaqbal Daily* in Beirut. He has also served as a cultural editor and contributor to other Lebanese national newspapers. His novels include *House of Mathilde*, *The Penguin's Song* and *Added Days*.

Mahmud Darwish was born in Palestine in 1941. He has published over twenty volumes of poetry, seven books of prose and has served as the editor of several publications. He currently resides between Ramallah and Amman.

Margaret Drabble, novelist, biographer and critic, was born in Sheffield in 1939. She is the editor of the fifth and sixth editions of *The Oxford Companion to English Literature* and was awarded the CBE in 1980.

Moris Farhi was born in Turkey. His latest novel is *Young Turk*. He is a vice-president of International PEN, and was awarded an MBE for services to literature. He lives in London.

Simone Fattal was born in Damascus, Syria in 1942. She is a painter and an art critic for Radio Lebanon. She moved to the US in 1980, where she founded the Post-Apollo Press, a publishing house specialising in poetry and experimental writing.

Robert Fisk is an author and Middle East correspondent for *The Independent*. He is currently reporting from Beirut.

Lara Frankena is a photographer and an editor at Saqi.

Maureen Freely grew up in Istanbul. She writes regularly for *The Guardian*, *Independent* and *Observer*, is the author of several works of fiction and non-fiction, and translated Orhan Pamuk's *Snow*.

Yasmine Gaspard spent her early childhood in Lebanon during the civil war. She is studying law with the aim of becoming a human rights lawyer. She doesn't believe in borders and hopes that one day humanity will learn to live in peace.

Maggie Gee has published many novels to great acclaim, including *The White Family* (2002), *The Flood* (2004) and *My Cleaner* (2005). Her most recent book is a collection of short stories, *The Blue* (2006). She is the first female Chair of the Royal Society of Literature.

Amal Ghandour is a research and communications strategist. She recently completed a memoir of the late Jordanian painter Ali al Jabri.

Mai Ghoussoub was born in Lebanon and moved to London in 1979. She is an artist, playwright and author of *Leaving Beirut* and *Imagined Masculinities*. She is a director of Saqi.

Charles Glass was Chief Middle East Correspondent of ABC News from 1983 to 1998. Hizbullah kidnapped him in Lebanon in 1987 and held him until he escaped two months later. His latest book is *The Northern Front*.

Cullen Goldblatt is a poet and translator who lives in New York. His translation of the book-length poem, *elobi*, by Cameroonian author Patrice Nganang, was published by Africa World Press in 2006.

Fabio Guzman is an Argentinean-born multimedia artist whose artwork and videos have been exhibited in numerous national and international festivals.

Malu Halasa is an editor and journalist. She is co-editor of *Creating Spaces of Freedom: Culture in Defiance* (2002), *Transit Beirut* (2004), and *The Secret Life of Syrian Lingerie: Intimacy and Design* (2007).

Mona Hatoum was born in Beirut in 1952, and moved to London in 1975. She has worked in the realm of performance, video and installation art since the early 1980s, and was nominated for the Turner Prize in 1995.

Tobias Hill was born in London in 1970. He is an award-winning poet and novelist. He was named as one of the Poetry Book Society's 'Next Generation' poets in 2004. His latest poetry collection is *Nocturne in Chrome and Sunset Yellow*.

Aamer Hussein was born in Karachi and moved to London in 1970. He reviews regularly for *The Independent* and the *TLS*. His fourth collection of short stories, *Insomnia*, will be published in 2007.

Nada Awar Jarrar was shortlisted for the Commonwealth Writers Prize 2004 for her novel *Somewhere, Home*. Her next novel, *Dreams of Water*, will be published next year. She currently lives in Lebanon with her husband and daughter.

Tahar Ben Jelloun was born in 1944 in Fez and emigrated to France in 1961. He has published numerous novels, collections of poetry, and essays. He was awarded the Prix Goncourt and the Prix Maghreb, and his novel *This Blinding Absence of Light* won the International IMPAC Award in 2004.

Judith Kazantzis has had several collections of poems published, most recently *The Odysseus Poems: Fictions on the Odyssey of Homer*. She has also published a novel, *Of Love and Terror*, several short stories, and is an established artist.

Peter Kennard is a painter, photographer, photomontage artist and senior tutor at the Royal College of Art. His *Dispatches from* *an Unofficial War Artist* charts his artistic, political and personal development.

Mazen Kerbaj was born in 1975 in Beirut, where he lives and works. He is a cartoonist, painter and musician, whose work can be seen on www.kerbaj.com.

Zena el-Khalil is an installation artist, painter, curator, and cultural and environmental activist. She is the co-founder of the art collective, xanadu*, which is based in New York and Beirut. She currently lives and works in Beirut.

Hanif Kureishi is an award-winning novelist, playwright, screenwriter and filmmaker. His most recent book *My Ear at His Heart* is about his father.

Doris Lessing was born in Persia in 1919 and spent her childhood in southern Africa, moving to England in 1949. She is widely regarded as one of the most important post-war writers in English.

Toby Litt is a novelist and short story writer; he also edited Henry James's last completed novel, *The Outcry*. In 2003 he was nominated by *Granta* magazine as one of the twenty 'Best of Young British Novelists'. He lives in London.

Hussein Madi was born in Chebaa in Lebanon in 1938. He is one of the Arab world's foremost artists. He lived in Rome for twenty-two years, but in 1987 he returned to live permanently in Lebanon. He has had more than sixty solo exhibitions worldwide.

Jean Said Makdisi is the author of *Beirut Fragments: A War Memoir*, and *Teta, Mother and Me: Three Generations of Arab Women*. She lives in Beirut.

Alberto Manguel is an anthologist, translator, essayist, novelist and editor, and is the author of several award-winning books. His book *With Borges* is published by Telegram.

Yann Martel was born in Salamanca, Spain, in 1963, of Canadian parents. His second novel *The Life of Pi* won the Man Booker Prize.

He is currently working on another novel, featuring a monkey and a donkey.

David Medalla was born in 1942 in Manila in the Phillipines and has lived in Britain, on and off, since the sixties. His work ranges from sculpture and kinetic art to painting, installation and performance.

Adrian Mitchell is a poet, playwright and writer of stories for children and adults. He has been a supporter of the peace movement all his life.

Blake Morrison was born in Yorkshire in 1950. Former Literary Editor of *The Observer* and *The Independent on Sunday*, he is an award-winning writer of fiction, poetry, plays and literary criticism.

Beverley Naidoo joined the resistance to apartheid as a student in South Africa. After detention without trial she came to England, into exile. Her writing has won many awards, including the Carnegie Medal. Her forthcoming book is *Burn My Heart*.

V. S. Naipaul was born in Trinidad in 1932. Novelist and author of a number of works of non-fiction, he was knighted in 1989 and won the Nobel Prize for Literature in 2001.

Alexandre Najjar was born in Lebanon in 1967. He is considered one of the best Lebanese novelists of his generation and is the recipient of many prizes. His latest book is *The School of War*. He is currently in Beirut.

Adam Nankervis is an Australian artist based in Liverpool and Berlin. He has exhibited extensively under the banner of museumMAN and has participated in the Los Angeles, Johannesburg and Liverpool biennials.

Greta Naufal is a Lebanese painter and video artist. She teaches fine art at the Lebanese American University and the American University of Beirut. Her work has been exhibited widely, and she was awarded the Sursock Prize for Painting and the Jury's Prize at the Biennale of Alexandria.

Shirin Neshat was born in Qazvin, Iran in 1957. She has had numerous solo shows of her photography and video work and has won several awards, including the First International Prize at the Venice Biennale. She lives in New York.

Rebecca O'Connor was born in Ireland in 1975. Her first collection of poetry, *Poems*, was published this year. She is an editor at Saqi.

Orhan Pamuk is one of Turkey's leading novelists. He has been translated into more than forty languages, and is the recipient of many international literary prizes.

Hadrian Piggott is an artist living and working in Cornwall. Recent work includes 'Elements of Drawing' for the Ashmolean Museum and a collaboration with the poet Hamish Robinson, which resulted in a book entitled *Rifiuti*, available from The Wordsworth Trust.

Harold Pinter, born in London in 1930, is a playwright, poet, actor, director and political activist. He was awarded the Nobel Prize for Literature in 2005.

Clare Pollard was born in 1978. She is a poet and playwright. She was the recipient of an Eric Gregory Award in 2000 and her first play, *The Weather*, was staged at the Royal Court in 2004. Her latest collection of poems is entitled *Look, Clare! Look!*

Hassan Ramadan was born in Leicester and grew up in Syria. He is Assistant Manager of the Arabic Department of Al Saqi Bookshop. He has worked as a translator for the BBC World Trust, and for various films, magazines and websites.

Mohammed Rawas was born in Beirut in 1951, and is considered one of Lebanon's leading artists. He has exhibited in the UK, Lebanon, Japan, Brazil, Tunisia and the US. He teaches at the American University in Beirut.

Rhea: 'The men slap their chests hysterically mourning the loss of a nation while the women dramatically weep and curse at random moments. Maybe Martha Stewart planned it. Three is the magic number. I live in a country whose tumour is out to get my neurons.

I'm a misanthrope and a vegetarian. Hippie, terrorist or the dancing queen, we're all the same. I could go on and on, but I'll end it here. My name? It's Rhea.'

Claudia Roden was born and brought up in Cairo. She has written many bestselling cookery books, including *The Book of Jewish Food*, which won the Wingate Prize for Non-Fiction.

Marisa Rueda was born in Buenos Aires, Argentina. A mixed-media and installation artist, she lives and works in London.

Hanan al-Shaykh was born in Beirut in 1945. Her most recent novel *Only in London* was shortlisted for the *Independent* Foreign Fiction Prize. She lives in London.

Kamila Shamsie was born in 1973 in Pakistan. Her second novel won her a place on Orange's list of '21 Writers for the 21st Century'. *Broken Verses* is her latest book.

Owen Sheers was born in 1974 in Suva Fiji, and brought up in London and South Wales. He is a poet, novelist and playwright. His latest collection *Skirrid Hill* was awarded the Somerset Maugham Prize.

anna sherbany: 'as an Iraqi-Jewish-Middle Eastern visual artist living in London I anna sherbany (am) negotiate(ing) issues of history, memory and location as well as race, class and gender.'

David Shrigley is an artist who lives and works in Glasgow. www.davidshrigley.com.

Iain Sinclair is an acclaimed British novelist, poet, essayist and filmmaker. His last book was *London Orbital*, describing a series of trips he took on foot around the M25, London's outer-ring motorway. Forthcoming is *London: City of Disappearances*.

Souheil Sleiman trained at the Royal College of Art, London and has been a practising sculptor since 1978. He has exhibited in group and solo shows in Britain and internationally.

Ali Smith was born in Inverness in 1962. She is a novelist and short story writer. Her last novel *The Accidental* won the 2005 Whitbread Novel Award.

George Szirtes was born in 1948 in Budapest and came to England as a refugee in 1956. He is a poet and translator, and has written sixteen plays, musicals, opera libretti and oratorios. His latest poetry collection *Reel* was awarded the T. S. Eliot Prize.

Arnold Wesker was born in London in 1942. He is the author of forty-two plays, four volumes of short stories, two volumes of essays, a book on journalism, a children's book, extensive journalism, poetry and other assorted writings.

Brian Whitaker is Middle East Editor of *The Guardian* newspaper. He recently launched his book *Unspeakable Love: Gay and Lesbian Life in the Middle East* in Beirut.

Hugo Williams is a poet, journalist and travel writer. He writes a column in the *Times Literary Supplement*, and his most recent poetry collection is *Dear Room*.

Anna Wilson is an editor and rights manager at Saqi.

Zapiro (Jonathan Shapiro) was born in Cape Town in 1958. He is Editorial Cartoonist for *The Mail* and *The Guardian*. He has published eight cartoon collections and has held solo exhibitions in New York, London, Frankfurt and throughout South Africa.